Praise for Monstress

"What I love about Tenorio's stories is the absence of nudge-nudge-wink-wink faux-irony that imbues so much contemporary fiction writing grounded in pop culture. The films of Ed Wood echo in the title story, and—in other stories—the Green Lantern and the Beatles and psychic surgery charlatanism and the grotesque circus of Jerry-Springeresque talk shows. But these are the backdrops for dramas that are profoundly human and humane. Outsiders and oddballs, outcasts and rejects—all are brought to vivid and affecting life in these stories. Tenorio never condescends, never goes for the easy joke or punch line. Tenorio's wit is understated; his writing is deft and self-assured; his dramas don't shout, but whisper, seductive and heartfelt. *Monstress* is one of the wisest and [most] heartfelt collections I've read. I've waited a long time for this book. To quote one of Tenorio's own characters: 'Jackpot—Eureka! This is the real deal.'"
—Daniel Orozco, author of *Orientation and Other Stories*

"In these fantastic stories, Tenorio skillfully blends the unlikely and the emotional, the bizarre and the humane. His writing portrays the universal human condition through unique specificity, and is very deserving of attention."
—Rishi Reddi, author of *Karma and Other Stories*

"*Monstress* is an exhilarating rollercoaster of a book. Deeply funny, heartbreaking, hopeful, philosophical, bawdy, and wise, Tenorio's stories, written from the underbelly of the American Dream, present one brilliant portrait after another."
—Sabina Murray, PEN/Faulkner Award–winning author of *The Caprices* and *Tales of the New World*

D0027861

MONSTRESS

To Vanessa —

Thanks for
reading!

— Lyd

MONSTRESS

STORIES

LYSLEY TENORIO

ecco

An Imprint of HarperCollins*Publishers*

Grateful acknowledgment is made to the following publications in which these stories first appeared, in slightly different form: "Monstress" and "L'amour, CA" in *The Atlantic;* "Superassassin" in *The Atlantic* and *Best New American Voices 2001;* "The Brothers" in *Manoa* and *The Pushcart Prize 2006;* "Felix Starro" in *Zoetrope: All-Story;* "The View from Culion" in *The Chicago Tribune;* "Help" in *Ploughshares* and *Broken Umbrella;* "Save the I-Hotel" in *Manoa* and *Best New American Voices 2010.*

HarperCollins books may be purchased for educational, business, or sales promotional use. For information, please e-mail the Special Markets Department at SPsales@harpercollins.com.

FIRST EDITION

Designed by Mary Austin Speaker

Library of Congress Cataloging-in-Publication Data has been applied for.

ISBN 978-0-06-205956-7

17 OV/RRD 10 9 8 7 6 5

for my mother,
Estrella Agojo Tenorio

and in memory of my father,
Pioquinto Gahol Tenorio

CONTENTS

MONSTRESS

Monstress

IN 1966, THE PRESIDENT OF COCOLOCO PICTURES broke the news to us in English: "As the Americanos say, it is time to listen to the music. Your movies are shit." He unrolled a poster for *The Squid Children of Cebu,* our latest picture for the studio. Our names were written in drippy, bloody letters: *A Checkers Rosario Film* was printed above the title, and my credit was at the bottom. *Reva Gogo,* it said, *as the Squid Mother.*

In its first week in release, *Squid Children* played in just one theater in all of Manila, the midnight show at the Primero. "A place for peasants and whores," the president said, tearing the poster in half, "and is it true they use a bedsheet for a screen?" Then, speaking in Tagalog, he fired us.

From CocoLoco we walked home, and when we passed the Oasis, one of the English-only movie theaters that had been sprouting up all over Manila, Checkers threw a stone at Doris Day's face: *Send Me No Flowers* was playing, and above the box office Doris Day and Rock Hudson traded sexy glances and knowing smiles. "Their fault!" he said, and I understood what he meant: imported Hollywood romance was what Manila moviegoers were paying to see, and Checkers' low-budget horror could no longer compete. "All that overacting, that corny shit!" But here was the truth: those were the movies I longed for Checkers to make, where men fall in love with women and stay there, and tearful partings are only preludes to tearful reunions. *Real life*—that's what I wanted to play, but my only roles were Bat-Winged Pygmy Queen, Werewolf Girl, Two-Headed Bride of Two-Headed Dracula, Squid Mother—all those monstrous girls Checkers dreamed up just for me.

I took the second stone from his hand and put it in my purse. "Time to go home," I said.

But we did not give up. Checkers shopped his latest (and last) screenplay, *Dino-Ladies Get Quezon City,* to all the Manila studios, even one in Guam; every answer was no. I auditioned and auditioned, and though casting agents liked my look (one called me a Filipina Sophia Loren), cold readings made me look like an amateur: I shouted dialogue that should have been whispered, and made tears of sorrow look like tears of joy.

For the next three years, this was our life: I worked as a receptionist at a dentist's office and Checkers lamented. One night, I woke to the sound of thwacking, and I found him drunk on the balcony, cracking open coconuts with a machete. "Was I no good?" he asked, his grunts turning to sniffles. I went to him, rested my head against the back of his neck. "Your chance will come again," I said. "But it's time for us to sleep."

Sometimes, when I play that night over in my head, I give it a new ending: I answer Checkers with the truth, that the most he ever achieved was minor local fame; that his movies were shoddily produced, illogically plotted, clumsily directed. This hurts Checkers—it hurts me, too—but the next morning we go on with our life, and I marvel at the possibilities: we might have married, there could have been children. We would still be together, and we wouldn't have needed Gaz Gazman, that Saturday morning in January of '70, when he rang our doorbell.

"Who are you?" I asked. Through the peephole I saw a stranger in a safari hat wipe his feet on our doormat as though we had already welcomed him.

"The name's Gazman. From Hollywood, USA. I'm here for a Checkers"—he looked at the name written on his palm—"Rosario."

I put my hand on the doorknob, made sure it was locked. "What do you want?"

He leaned into the peephole, his smile so big I caught the glint of a shiny gold crown on a back tooth. "His monsters," he said.

From the bedroom I heard Checkers start his day the usual way, with a phlegmy cough from the previous night's bourbon. I went to him. "Someone is here," I said, poking his shoulder. "From Hollywood."

He lifted his head.

I returned to the front door. I didn't want to, but I did. For Checkers. I unlocked the lock and let Gaz Gazman in.

I led him to the kitchen, offered him a plate of Ritz crackers and a square of margarine. I stood by the sink, watching him as he ate: his shirt and shorts were covered with palm trees, and his purple sandals clashed with the orange lenses of his sunglasses. A large canvas bag was on the floor beside him, and his hat was still on.

Checkers stepped into the kitchen. "The great Checkers Rosario," Gaz said.

Checkers stared at Gaz with bloodshot eyes. "Used to be," he said, then sat down.

Gaz explained himself: he was in Manila visiting an ex-girlfriend, a makeup artist for CocoLoco. He had toured the studio, gone through their vaults, and found copies of Checkers' movies. "I watched them all, and I thought, *Jackpot—Eureka! This is the real deal.* They said if I wanted to use them, I should find you." He pulled four canisters of film from his canvas bag and stacked them on the table. "And now you're found."

Checkers took the reels from the canisters. I could hear him whisper their titles like the names of women he once loved and still did—*The Creature in the Cane, Cathedral of Dread, DraculaDracula, The House on Dead Filipino Road.* "Use them," he said. "What for?"

"Three words," Gaz said. "Motion. Picture. History." He got up, circled the table as he explained his movie: en route to Earth from a distant star system, the crew of the

Valedictorian crash-lands on a hostile planet inhabited by bat-winged pygmies, lobster-clawed cannibals, two-headed vampires. "That's where your stuff comes in. I'm going to splice your movies with mine." He went on about the mixing-up of genres, chop-suey cinema, bringing together East and West. "We'd be the ambassadors of international film!"

"What's your thinking on this?" Checkers asked me in Tagalog. "Is this man serious? Is he just an American fool?"

"Ask how much he'll pay," I said, "get twenty percent more, give him the movies, and show him to the door."

"All our hard work for a few pesos?" Checkers looked at me as though I'd slapped him. "That's their worth to you?" He asked if I'd forgotten the ten-star reviews, the long lines on opening night, but I didn't want to hear about it, not anymore, so I reminded him about the life we'd been living the last three years—how I sat day after day in an un-air-conditioned dentist's office, staring at a phone that never rang, while he slept through hangovers into the late afternoon, only to reminisce about our CocoLoco days throughout the night. "Take the money," I said, "and let's be done with this."

"I come in peace!" Gaz said. "Don't fight because of me."

I switched back to English. "We are discussing, not fighting. We don't have lawyers or agents to counsel us over these matters. There is corruption and dishonesty in the movie business here in Manila. It's not like in Hollywood."

"But I'm one of the good guys," Gaz said, and to prove

it, he made us an offer: "Come to America. Just for a week. You can see a rough cut, visit the set, meet the cast. Plenty of room at my pad. I'll even take the couch. And if you don't like what you see, I'll reimburse you the airfare and you won't ever hear from me again."

Then Checkers said, "Reva will come too."

I shook my head. "This is your business." I spoke in English, so that Gaz would understand me too. "The two of you. Not the three of us."

"But I need you," Checkers said. He came to me and held my face, then kissed me just above my nose.

Gaz winked at me. "How can you say no to that?"

There was a smudge of gray just above Checkers' lip, like dried-up toothpaste or cigarette ash. I licked my thumb, rubbed it away. His shirt was misbuttoned at the top, there were patches of stubble he missed when he shaved, and his Elvis-style pompadour showed more gray than I'd realized was there.

"I can't," I told Gaz.

"SOMEONE IN AMERICA IS DEAD." This was the lie I told the dentist when I asked for a week off from work. "Someone close to me." It was easy to say—I told him over the phone—but part of me hoped he would deny my request. If I had to stay, maybe Checkers would, too. But the dentist said my presence made no difference, that no one could afford dental work these days, so maybe we were all better off if we simply went away. He wished me a happy trip and hung up before I could say thank you.

We left Monday morning, and our flight to California felt like backwards travel through time. In Manila it was night but outside the plane the sky was packed with clouds so white they looked fake, like the clouds painted on the cinderblock walls of the Primero. Checkers and I began our courtship there, thirteen years before. I was sixteen, he was twenty-two, and every Saturday night we held hands in the second row at the midnight double creature feature. Checkers would marvel at what he called "the beauty of the beast," confirming the expert craftsmanship of a well-made monster with a quiet "Yes" (he gave a standing ovation to the Creature from the Black Lagoon) and let out exasperated sighs for the lesser ones. But I preferred the monster that could be tamed. Like Fay Wray, I wanted to lie on the leathery palm of my gorilla suitor, soothe his rage with my calming, loving gaze. "You'll be on-screen one day," Checkers said. "I'll put you there. Just keep faith in me."

So I did. After high school, I moved in with Checkers, took odd jobs sewing and cleaning while he worked on his treatment for *The Creature in the Cane*. The night Coco-Loco Pictures bought it, Checkers gave me a white box tied with pink ribbon. "Wear this," he whispered. "For me." I expected a nightgown with a broken strap and tattered neckline—standard attire for a woman in peril—but when I opened it I found a pair of wolf ears, a rubber forehead covered with boils, several plastic eyeballs. "You will be the Creature," he said, near tears and smiling. "You."

The night we started filming, as I rubber-glued eyeballs to my face, I told myself this was a first step, that even great actresses have unglamorous starts. I told myself this again the night of the premiere, when audiences cheered wildly as a dozen sugarcane farmers descended upon the Creature with sticks and buckets of holy water. *This is only the beginning*—I repeated, like a prayer, through all the films I did for Checkers.

For nearly the entire flight over, Checkers slept with his head resting on my chest, but our landing was so rough and jolting that he woke in a panic, and his head slammed hard against my chin. "We're here?" he said, breathing heavy. "Have we finally arrived?" I rubbed the back of his neck to calm him. But my lip was bleeding. I could taste it.

GAZ DIDN'T LIVE IN HOLLYWOOD. He lived east of it, in Los Feliz, in a gray building called the Paradise. "This is it," he said, unlocking the door, "the home of Gaz Gazman and DoubleG Productions." It was a tiny apartment furnished with a sinking couch and a pair of yellow beanbags, and the offices of DoubleG Productions were a walk-in closet with a metal desk crammed inside, a telephone and a student film trophy—second place—on top of it. A junior college diploma hung above the fake fireplace, and it was then that I learned Gaz Gazman was not his real name. "Who the hay wants to see a movie by Gazwick Goosmahn? But *Gaz Gazman*"—he snapped twice—"that's a director's name."

"It's the same with me!" Checkers said. "My real name? Chekiquinto. Can you believe?" He shook his head and laughed. "*Chekiquinto*. My gosh!"

"Horrible!" Gaz laughed along. "And you? Is Reva Gogo for real?" He said it like he already knew that it wasn't. My real name was Revanena Magogolang, but Checkers thought all the repetitive syllables made my name sound like a tongue twister, so right before *The Creature in the Cane* was released, he de-clunked it down to its smoothest sound. *And Reva Gogo,* my credit read, *as the Creature.*

I took Checkers' hand and made him sit with me on a beanbag. "Show us your movie," I said. The sooner we saw Gaz's clips, I thought, the sooner we could get our money and fly home.

Gaz wheeled in a film projector from his bedroom, loaded a 16 millimeter reel, then hung a white bedsheet on the wall. "There are rough spots," he said, "but I think you'll like what you see." He drew the curtains, turned off the lights, filled a bowl with pretzels, then showed us the footage he'd completed so far.

The film opened with a view of Earth from outer space, and a voice (Gaz's) began: *"The year is 1999. The world and all its good citizens have never been better. World peace has been achieved, no child goes hungry, disease has been gotten rid of. Man is free to contemplate the human condition, and, more importantly, colonize outer space."* Entering the picture was a bottle-shaped spaceship, THE

VALEDICTORIAN glittering in blue letters along its hull. "There she is," Gaz whispered, "the smartest ship in the fleet." A whistle blew, and then a weird, psychedelic montage of oddly angled stills began: there was Captain Vance Banner, the square-jawed fearless leader; Ace Trevor, the hotheaded helmsman; the Intelli-Bot 4-26-35 ("My birthday," Gaz said); and finally Lorena Valdez, the raven-haired, olive-skinned meteor scientist. "Eyes darker than the cosmic void, lips redder than human blood," Gaz quoted from his script.

Gaz loaded a second reel, quick scenes of the actors running in a nearby canyon, which would be the planet inhabited by Checkers' monsters. "That's where I'll splice your footage in," Gaz said. The canyon scenes were composed of reaction shots, extreme close-ups of the actors shouting, *"Look out!" "Duck, Captain, duck!"* and *"They're hideous!"* "I had them take expressions lessons in West Hollywood." Gaz said. "They've definitely done their homework."

I looked at Checkers. There were pretzel crumbs on the corner of his mouth, but when I tried to wipe them off he brushed my hand away. "Ssshh," he said. His face glowed blue from the movie on the wall, as it once did back in the CocoLoco editing room, late at night after a long day's shoot. I would end up asleep on the floor, and when I woke the next morning he'd still be in his chair, struggling to make every scene as perfect as it could be.

Gaz turned off the projector. "And that's just the beginning." He smiled. "So, are we in?"

Even before Gaz turned on the lights, Checkers was on

his feet. "Let's do it," he said. His breathing was heavy and fast, almost desperate, and his forehead was drippy with sweat. "I'm ready," he said, "we're in."

IT WAS STILL EARLY EVENING, and Gaz suggested we drive to the set. "MGM?" Checkers guessed. "Twentieth Century-Fox?"

"My mom's basement in Pasadena," Gaz answered.

Freeway traffic was slow; I fell asleep in the backseat, and when I woke we were in front of Gaz's mother's house. It was an old, peeling Victorian with a shingled roof that had almost no shingles left, and the shutters dangled from the uppermost windows, like limbs attached to a body by one last vein. That house would have been Checkers' dream set. We'd had to make do with tin-roofed shacks and three-walled huts in shantytowns far beyond Manila, where we paid impoverished locals with cigarettes and sacks of rice to play our victims for a day. "If we'd had something like this to work with," Checkers said, "life back home would still be good."

The basement was like an underground studio set, sectioned off by plywood partitions and cardboard walls: each room was a different section of *The Valedictorian*—the bridge, the science lab, the weapons bay, the space sauna. We hadn't been on a set since *Squid Children* five years before, but Checkers made himself at home, examining each room from different angles, as though he were behind a camera, filming right then.

I wandered off alone. "Explore all you want, but don't touch anything," Gaz said. But I didn't need to touch anything to know its cheapness: the helm was made of Styrofoam and cardboard, painted to look like steel; the main computer was a reconfigured pinball machine; the Intelli-Bot 4-26-35 was an upside-down fishbowl painted gold atop a small TV set, and its bottom half was a vacuum cleaner on wheels. But I was used to this lack of marvelousness, because Checkers worked this way too, attempting magic from junk: wet toilet tissue shaped like fangs was good enough for a wolf-man or vampire, and our ghosts were just bedsheets. For the Squid Children, Checkers found a box of fireman's rubber boots, glued homemade tentacles (segments of rubber hose affixed with suction cups) on them, then made his tiny nephews and nieces wear them on their heads. "On film," Checkers used to say, "everything looks real."

I found Checkers and Gaz in the space lab, the contract between them: Gaz would pay twenty-five hundred dollars up front, then pay five percent of the profits. "Jackpot-Eureka!" Checkers said after he signed, though neither of us knew how much that would be worth back home.

GAZ AND CHECKERS WANTED TO celebrate, so we went from bar to bar on Hollywood Boulevard, then strolled along the Walk of Fame. "A trio of visionaries should have the stars at their feet, right, Chex?" Gaz said. Checkers nodded, zigzagging down the street. For so long, Checkers had resented Hollywood, convinced it was American movies that drove us out of the business. Now, here he was, lolling about in enemy territory, drunk from beer, bourbon, and all the inspiration surrounding him—the Hollywood Wax Museum, Grauman's Chinese Theatre, even the life-size celebrity cutouts in storefront windows. I tried keeping up, making sure he didn't fall.

Hours later, Checkers and I made love on Gaz's couch. At first I told him we shouldn't, not there in a stranger's home. "He's so drunk he'll never wake up," Checkers assured me. He nibbled my neck and nuzzled my breasts, let out a low guttural growl. "Gently," I said, running my fingers through his pompadour, "softly." He obeyed. I knew Checkers was drunk, but this was how I wanted us to finish the day: it was the longest of our lives, thirty-seven hours since we left Manila. So I gave myself up to this moment when we could finally slow down, and I imagined us as Deborah Kerr and Burt Lancaster in *From Here to Eternity*.

THE NEXT MORNING I REACHED for Checkers and he wasn't there. I opened my eyes and found him on the floor, asleep on his stomach. For a moment I thought we were in Manila again, that this was just another of our ordinary days. But then I saw the yellow beanbags on the floor, brighter than anything in our apartment back home.

I got dressed and went into the kitchen. Gaz was already

there, sunglasses on, wearing a tiger-print robe. "Now that," he said, standing by the window, "is a Hollywood morning." I looked out. Everything was hazy and bright at the same time.

Suddenly I realized Gaz was staring at me. "What?"

"It's weird to see you this way. In the human flesh, I mean." He removed his sunglasses. "I remember you in Checkers' movies, all fancy with your tentacles and boils and lobster claws. Chex got lucky when he found you. You make a good monster. You're a mistress of monsters." He chuckled. "You're a monstress."

"I am not monstrous," I said.

"Mon*stress*," he said. "Not mon*strous*. See for yourself." He looked behind and above me. I turned around, and then I saw it, tacked to the wall: a poster for *The Squid Children of Cebu*. "I swiped it from CocoLoco, hung it up this morning. Thought it might make you two feel at home."

The edges had yellowed, but the picture was still clear: a dozen Squid Children on the edge of a lagoon, and behind them, lying on the shore, is the Squid Mother, her belly bloated with squid eggs yet to be spawned, tentacles flailing. That costume was sticky and rubbery, but by the end of the day it felt like my own skin. For hours I would roll along the dirty sand, moaning, "Grraarggh, grraargh," and I remember thinking, *This is it, this is my life,* as Checkers filmed me from afar. I hadn't seen the poster since the president of CocoLoco showed it to us, as an example of our failure.

. . .

AT NOON, WE RETURNED TO the set to meet the cast. It was trash collection day in Pasadena; garbage cans lined the street, and in front of Gaz's mother's house, the parts of a dismantled mannequin lay in a pile on the sidewalk. "We can use this," Gaz said. "Help me out, Chex."

I walked ahead of them, toward the back of the house. The basement door was open. "Hello?" I called out. I stepped inside, heard giggling coming from the bridge. When I turned the corner I found Captain Banner and Ace Trevor leaning against the helm, their arms around each other. They might have been kissing. "Sorry," I said, my face warm from embarrassment.

They let go of each other, stood up straight. "We were just going over lines." The man who played Captain Banner held out his hand. "Everett Noel Dubois. But friends call me E. Noel. This is Prescott St. John, a.k.a. Ace Trevor." Prescott smiled, straightening his collar. They were the first professional actors I'd met in years, and I worried they would ask about my own acting history; a list of my roles and movies formed in my head, and they made me feel meager, shameful. I wanted to avoid the subject altogether, focus only on the good parts of my life. "I work for a dentist in Manila" was all I could think to say.

Gaz and Checkers walked in, carrying legs, arms, a torso. They set the mannequin parts on the ground, and Gaz made formal introductions. "Where's our Lorena?" he asked, looking at his watch. "If it's one thing I demand from my actors," he said, "it's punctuality. Be back in a flash." He went upstairs to call her at home. E. Noel and Prescott went outside to go over lines.

Checkers knelt to the floor and started rebuilding the mannequin. He said he was genuinely impressed by what he'd seen so far, but then he whispered his disappointments in Tagalog. "His camera work is unsteady," he said. "And his composition is so-so. But I have some suggestions for him. Lucky for him I have the experience, right?" He looked up at me. "What? Why is your face like that?"

"Like what?"

"Like this." He scrunched up his face into a girlish pout and rolled his eyes. "What's wrong with you?"

I knelt down beside him. "Maybe we should go home today. Just take the twenty-five hundred before he changes his mind."

"Is your head broken? We have almost a week left. The American will need my guidance. This is a Gazman-Rosario Production, don't you know?"

I slammed the mannequin hand against the ground; the pinkie finger broke off. "'Gazman-*Rosario* Production?' Gazman-*Idiot* Production! You've already done the work he needs. You finished it years ago!" I took a deep breath, made my voice gentle again. "You were finished years ago. Don't start this nonsense again. If you do . . ." I should have stopped there, but the poster in Gaz's kitchen hung in my head like a fateful welcome-home banner, and I couldn't go back. "If you do, I won't forgive you this time."

Checkers set the mannequin's right arm on the ground.

Then he got to his feet, took backwards steps toward the wall, the way my victims would in his movies, right before the kill. "Checkers." I held my arms out to comfort him, but he wouldn't come to me. "Checkers?"

Suddenly there was cursing and shouting as Gaz came running down the stairs. "Crap!" he said. He kicked a computer console and it flew across the basement. "I lost my Lorena Valdez! She decided she'd rather do some bimbo role for a guy named Roman What's-His-Face than finish my movie." He leaned against the wall, slid down to the floor, put his face on his knees. "Where am I going to find another actress who'll work for free? Crap!"

Then Checkers started pacing too. "Crap-crap!" he shouted. He went on about the money he would lose, and he wondered how someone who once was great could slip away into a life as dead-end as ours. "I'm sorry," I said, reaching for him. But he just pushed my arm away, told me to leave him alone. So I went to Gaz instead, and patted his shoulder to calm him down. This was the end of things, I was sure of it; the loss of Lorena Valdez was a sign that this collaboration was never meant to be, and it was time for Checkers and me to return to our real life back home.

Gaz inhaled deeply through his nose and exhaled through his mouth several times, then took my hand from his shoulder and squeezed it tight. His head rose slowly and he stared into my eyes, almost lovingly. I thought he might try to kiss me, so I freed my hand from his and stepped back.

"What size space suit do you wear?" he whispered.

. . .

I NEVER WANTED TO BE Lorena Valdez. But Gaz insisted that I was born to play her, and besides, this was the only way to guarantee the deal he'd made with Checkers. "Think of the money," Gaz said, and though Checkers stayed silent, I finally agreed that it was the only thing to do.

It was 102 degrees the day we started filming. We were at the bottom of a canyon in Los Feliz, and all morning long, E. Noel, Prescott, and I ran back and forth, pretending to flee from Checkers' monsters, while Gaz followed us with a handheld camera. Checkers was alone at the top of the canyon by the NO TRESPASSING sign, looking out for cops.

At noon, we filmed a crucial scene that required me to run up the side of the canyon. "Now you're fleeing from the stinkiest, oogiest, bat-winged pygmy you've ever seen," Gaz said, "and it wants you for breakfast." He put his hands on my shoulders, leaned in close. "Think about that as you're running away. Understand?"

I had never taken direction from another man before. "I do," I said.

Gaz set up the camera at the bottom of the canyon, then called action. I ran. I visualized myself from years before, chasing after me now, fangs bared and claws ready to shred, tentacles wrapping around me, squeezing me to my final breath. I could hear a hiss in my ear, and I shivered in the heat. I ran faster, staggering uphill on my hands and knees, telling myself, *Climb. Get to safety.* But when I looked up I saw

Checkers walking toward me, as though he was trying to sabotage the shot. "Go!" I whispered. "You're ruining the picture!" For a moment Checkers looked confused, like he suddenly realized he had no idea where he was, but finally backed away.

I reached the top. I got to my feet, looked straight down into the camera, and screamed my very first line of dialogue ever: *"They're hideous!"* Then Gaz yelled cut, clapped twice, and proclaimed Lorena Valdez a new heroine for our time.

THE DAY BEFORE I WAS meant to leave America, we shot the love scene. "Hold her here," Gaz directed. He placed E. Noel's hands on the small of my back, then put my arms around E. Noel's neck. He stepped back, checked the shot.

It wasn't cold in Gaz's mother's basement, but I was shaking. "You seem nervous," E. Noel whispered. "First on-screen kiss?"

I had gouged, bitten, clawed, stabbed. Never kissed. "No."

He smiled, like he didn't believe me. "Well, if you do get nervous, just pretend I'm Checkers."

Gaz called action. We started the scene.

We spoke of our failed mission and our fallen comrades—Ace had been barbecued by the bat-winged pygmies, and the Intelli-Bot 04-26-35 had malfunctioned beyond repair and turned against us —and we spoke of time wasted harnessing comet-tail energy, studying asteroid samples, mining moons for precious metals. *"All that matters to me now,"* E. Noel said, *"is you."*

"Captain," I said. *"I—I'm frightened."*

"Of what? That demonic intergalactic menagerie of fanged creatures can't touch us. Not now. Not with only five minutes of oxygen left."

"No. That's not it. I'm afraid of"—I took a deep breath— *"of loving you. Meteor analysis, moon colonization, those things are easy. But not love. Love takes work. Love takes time and we're running out of it."* I broke free from E. Noel's embrace, walked toward the observation window, in near-disbelief that these lines, the most beautiful I had ever spoken, were actually mine.

E. Noel put his hands on my shoulders. *"Lorena. Of all the star systems I have explored, of every planet upon which I've walked, there is nowhere in the galaxy I'd rather be than here, on the bridge of* The Valedictorian, *looking into your eyes. If this is my end, then it's more than I could have ever hoped for."* He pulled me close against him.

"I don't know what—"

He put his index finger over my mouth. *"Ssshh. Just kiss me, Lorena. That's an order."*

The slick of saliva and flesh of his lips. The running of his fingers through my wig. Our chests and hearts coming together. It all thrilled me, knowing the camera was there to capture the moment.

Then someone started laughing.

"Cut!" Gaz shouted. "What the dang is so funny?"

It was Checkers. "Pardon," he said, smirking. "Sorry."

I let go of E. Noel. I walked off the bridge, toward Checkers. "What's wrong with you?"

"With me?" Checkers said in Tagalog. "Do you know what you look like up there? All that corny talk. All that overacting the American is making you do." He shook his head, started laughing again.

"That's enough," I said. But he kept going, and his laughter turned to cruelty: he said the scene between Lorena and Banner was utterly unbelievable, that no two people would say such meaningless things in what could be the last moments of their lives. "They would try to stay alive. They would fight. That's what brave explorers of outer space do, right?" He belittled Gaz's script, insulted my acting, poked fun at the fact that I was kissing an obvious homosexual. "On film," he said, "you will look like a whore."

Sometimes I wonder if he meant this as a warning, a last chance to save me from starring in yet another fool's movie. I didn't think this at the time. Instead, my hand went up, then lashed forward, a gesture I'd made dozens of times before in Checkers' films, and the other actor always knew the precise moment to duck. But this time, I made actual contact and inflicted real pain: I slapped Checkers hard across the face, and my nails left red scratches just below his eye. "Get away from here," I said.

Checkers touched his face. He looked at the blood on his fingers.

"Get off the set," I said it in English, so that everyone around could understand me, "and let me act." Checkers moved away, still stunned, then left the basement.

Gaz called places. "From the top," he said. We began again, but E. Noel kept stumbling over *"demonic intergalactic menagerie,"* and there were technical difficulties on the fifth, sixth, seventh takes. Only on the eleventh did we finally get it right: I took E. Noel's advice and pretended he was Checkers. When we kissed, I managed to shed one single, perfect tear, just as Gaz had written in the script.

"SLIGHT PROBLEMO," GAZ SAID THE next day. "We're not done." Checkers and I were packing for our flight back home. We hadn't spoken since I struck him, and he did not return to Gaz's apartment until early that morning. To this day, I don't know where he was the previous night, or how he found his way back.

Gaz explained the situation: "You're in the shot, Chex. When Lorena's running up the canyon, you're standing right there like this." He got up, put his hands in his pockets, and looked around like a lost tourist. "I could try to write you into the script, but at this point"—Gaz sat down, started folding one of Checkers' shirts—"I need you to stay." He was speaking to me. "A day or two, maybe three. There are some other scenes I'd like to reshoot. I'll even pay for your new ticket back. What do you say?"

. . .

HOURS LATER, WE DROPPED CHECKERS off at the curb. "Happy trails," Gaz said, patting Checkers on the back, "till we meet again."

Checkers stared at Gaz for a few seconds, the way he did the morning they met, then got out of the car. "Five percent," he said. "Don't forget."

I walked with Checkers to the entrance. "You'll be okay, right?" I said. "It's just a few days." I fixed his collar, smoothed his hair. I leaned in to kiss him goodbye, but stopped at the sight of the scratch marks on his face. They had scabbed over, and I traced over them with my finger. "Fool," I said, shaking my head and weeping, "look what you made me do." He grabbed hold of my wrist, put my hand to his lips, and instead of kissing it, he simply breathed in through his nose and mouth, as though I were air to him, his only oxygen. Then he let me go and went inside.

Gaz handed me a tissue when I got back in the car. "What's a few days?" he said. What he couldn't understand was that Checkers and I had never left one another before, and on the way to the airport, I'd daydreamed for us a lovelier farewell scene: just before takeoff Checkers exits the plane, dashes across the tarmac to get to me. We kiss so long and hard, hold each other so tight, that there is no way we can ever be apart.

GAZ FINALLY TITLED THE MOVIE *The Terror of the Fanged Creatures*, and the morning after we finished shooting, Gaz showed me the screenplay for his next movie, *Pasadena RollerWars*. "I'm still looking for my BB San Juan," he said. "The tough and sexy heroine of the deadliest rink in town. Think it over." I called Checkers and told him all the things Gaz told me: that once-in-a-lifetime opportunities really are once-in-a-lifetime, that another American role would be good for my career, that we could always use the money. "I'm doing this for us, right?" I said.

There was a moment of silence on Checkers' end. I thought we had been disconnected. "CocoLoco wants me back," he finally said. "They read *Dino-Ladies Get Quezon City* and they want me to direct it. They said if my old movies can conquer Hollywood, then my new ones can double-conquer Manila. It's unlucky for you that you're not around to star in it."

I had burned the only copy of *Dino-Ladies* years before, but I let Checkers talk his talk, because it was better than the truth—I could see him sitting on the couch, in his boxer shorts and dirty undershirt, waiting amidst his mess for my return. "Your chance came again," I said, "congratulations." Then I hung up, found Gaz sitting in his kitchen staring at the Hollywood morning, and told him yes.

After *RollerWars*, I did two more films for Gaz: *The Twisted History-Mystery* and *Jesse: Girl of a Thousand Streets*. Altogether, they took almost three years to shoot. Checkers and I spoke less, rarely returned each other's calls, and I learned not to miss him by reminding myself that I was a working, professional actress in America; back home, I didn't know what I was. I never returned to find out.

But of all the films I did for Gaz, only *Fanged Creatures* is remembered. I saw it again, just last year at the Silver Scream Theater in L.A., almost twenty years after its original release. I sat alone in the second row; behind me an audience of college students mocked and hooted throughout, laughing especially hard during my kiss with E. Noel. But that scene still moved me—what did those young people know about the world ending all around you?

Overall, *Fanged Creatures* was still impressive: the plot was fast-paced, the camerawork was steady, and our reaction shots conveyed all the fear and dread Gaz hoped for. But the back-and-forth shifts between his film and Checkers' footage was rougher than I remembered: bright Technicolor pictures alternated with yellowish, grainy ones, and Checkers' monsters moved in a dreamy slow motion: the Squid Mother's tentacles flowed around her like the tails of kites, the Bat-Winged Pygmy Queen glided through the air like a leaf in the wind, Werewolf Girl looked almost lovely as she bayed at the moon. It had been so long since I had seen myself this way that I was secretly mournful at the end when, after Captain Banner manages to restore power to the engines, Lorena presses the button that drops the nucleotomic bombs on Planet X. "There you are," Gaz whispered to me, the night of its premiere, "obliterating yourselves out of existence."

But what stayed with me then, what loops in my head even now, is what I didn't see in the movie: that scene in the canyon, the one Gaz said Checkers ruined. I saw it only once, right before Gaz edited it out: on hands and knees I struggle uphill, a filthy, sweaty mess—my wig is a nest of pebbles and leaves, dirt smears my face, neck, and space suit. But it makes no difference to Checkers. He comes to me with open arms, like I am a thing of unequaled beauty. *On film, everything looks real.* It was true: it did look like Checkers meant to help me up, to pull me to safety, and rescue me from that most hostile of planets.

The Brothers

MY BROTHER WENT ON NATIONAL TV TO PROVE HE was a woman. I don't know which talk show it was, but the episode had a title that kept flashing at the bottom of the television screen: IS SHE A HE? IS HE A SHE? YOU DECIDE! The show went like this: a guest would come out onstage, and the audience would vote on whether or not she was the real thing.

They came out one at a time, these big-haired and bright-lipped women, most of them taller than the average man. They worked the stage like strippers, bumping and grinding to the techno beat of the background music. The audience was on its feet, whistling and hooting, cheering them on.

Then came Eric.

My brother was different from the others. He was shorter, the only Filipino among them. He wore a denim skirt and a T-shirt, a pair of Doc Martens. His hair, a few strands streaked blond, fell to his bony shoulders. He was slow across the stage, wooing the audience with a shy girl's face, flirtatious, sweet. But he wasn't woman enough for them: they booed my brother, gave him the thumbs-down. So Eric fought back. He stood at the edge of the stage, fists on his hips and feet shoulder-width apart, like he was ready to take on anyone who crossed him. "Dare me?" he said, and I saw his hands move slowly to the bottom of his T-shirt. "You dare me?"

They did, and up it went. The crowd screamed with approval, gave him the thumbs-up. Someone threw a bra onstage and Eric picked it up, twirled it over his head like a lasso, then flung it back into the audience.

I looked over at Ma. It was like someone had hit her in the face.

He put his shirt down, lifted his arms in triumph, blew kisses to the audience, then took a seat with the others. He told the audience that his name was Erica.

He'd left a message the night before it aired, telling me to watch Channel 4 at seven o'clock that night. He said it would be important, that Ma should see it too. When I told Ma she looked hopeful. "Maybe he's singing," she said, "playing the piano?" She was thinking of Eric from long before, when he took music lessons and sang in the high school choir.

I reached for the remote, thinking, *That bastard set us up.* I turned off the TV.

That was the last time I saw Eric. Now he's lying on a table, a sheet pulled to his shoulders. The coroner doesn't rush me, but I answer him quickly. "Yes," I say. "That's my brother."

. . .

ERIC'S LIFE WAS NO SECRET, though we often wished it was: we knew about the boyfriends, the makeup and dresses. He told me about his job at the HoozHoo, a bar in downtown San Francisco where the waitresses were drag queens and transsexuals. But a year and a half ago, on Thanksgiving night, when Eric announced that he was going to proceed with a sex change ("Starting here" he said, patting his chest with his right hand), Ma left the table and told Eric that he was dead to her.

It's 6:22 P.M. He's been dead for six hours.

"We need to call people," I tell Ma. But she just sits there at the kitchen table, still in her waitress's uniform, whispering things to herself, rubbing her thumb along the curve of Eric's baby spoon. Next week she turns sixty-one. For the first time, she looks older than she is. "We have to tell people what's happened."

She puts down the spoon, finally looks at me. "What will I say? How can I tell it?"

"Tell them what the coroner told me. That's all." He had an asthma attack, rare and fatal. He was sitting on a bench in Golden Gate Park when his airways swelled so quickly, so completely, no air could get in or out. As a kid, Eric's asthma was a problem; I can still hear the squeal of his panic. *Can't breathe, can't breathe,* he'd say, and I'd rub his back and chest like I was giving him life. But as an adult, the attacks became less frequent, easier to manage, and he deemed his inhaler a thing of the past. "The severity of this attack was unusual," the coroner explained. "No way he could have prepared for it." He was dead by the time a pair of ten-year-olds on Rollerblades found him.

The look on her face makes me feel like I'm a liar. "He couldn't breathe," I say. "It's the truth." I go through cupboards, open drawers, not sure what I'm looking for, so I settle for a mug and fill it with water and though I'm not thirsty I drink it anyway. "He couldn't breathe. And then he died. When people ask, that's what you say."

Ma picks up the spoon again, and now I understand: *"Ang bunso ko,"* she's been saying. My baby boy, over and over. Like Eric died as a child and she realized it only now.

THE MORNING AFTER THE SHOW, my brother called me at work. When I picked up, he said, "Well . . . ?" like we were in mid-conversation, though we hadn't spoken in six months.

"You grew your hair out," I said. "It's blond now."

"Extensions," he said.

"They look real."

"They're not." He took a deep breath. "But the rest of me is."

It was a little after seven. I was the only one in the office. Not even the tech guys were in yet. I turned and looked out my window, down at the street, which was empty too.

"Goddamnit, Edmond," my brother said. "Say something."

I didn't, so he did. He said he was sorry if it hurt Ma and me, but this was a once-in-a-lifetime opportunity. "I showed the world what I'm made of." He said this slowly, like it was a line he'd been rehearsing for months. "What do you think of that?"

"I saw nothing," I said.

"What?"

"I saw nothing." It was the truth. When Eric lifted his shirt, they didn't simply cover his breasts with a black rectangle. They didn't cut to commercial or pan the camera to a shocked face in the audience. Instead, they blurred him out, head to toe. It looked like he was disintegrating, molecule by molecule. "They blurred you out," I said.

I could hear him pace his apartment. I'd never visited, but I knew he was living in the Tenderloin in downtown San Francisco. The few times he called, there were always things happening on his end—cars honking, sirens, people shouting and laughing. But that morning, there was just the sound of us breathing, one, then the other, like we were taking turns. I imagined a pair of divers at the bottom of the ocean, sharing the same supply of air.

"You there?" I finally said. "Eric, are you there?"

"No," he said, then hung up.

And that's how it ended, for Eric and me.

I GO TO MY APARTMENT to get clothes, but stay the night at Ma's. My old bed is still in my old room upstairs, but I take the living room couch. I don't sleep, not for a minute. Before light comes, I call Delia in Chicago, but her fiancé picks up. I ask for my wife, which irritates him. But technically, I'm right: the divorce isn't final, not yet. I'm still her husband, and I won't let that go, not until I have to.

"No message," I tell him, then hang up.

Somehow, I'm wide awake all morning. Driving to the funeral home in North Oakland, I don't even yawn.

Loomis, the man who handled Dad's funeral eleven years ago, waits for us in a small square of shade outside the main office. He's heavier now, his hair thinner, all white. Back then he walked with a limp; today he walks with a cane.

"Do you remember me?" It's the first thing Ma says to him. "And my husband?" She pulls a picture from her wallet, an old black-and-white of Dad back in his Navy days. He's wearing fatigues, looking cocky. His arms hang at his sides, but his fists are clenched, like he's ready for a fight. "Dominguez. First name Teodoro." Loomis takes the photo, holds it eye level, squints. "I do remember him," he says, though he saw my father only as a corpse. "And I remember you too." He looks at me, shakes my hand. "The boy who never left his mother's side that whole time."

That was Eric. Ma knows it too. We don't correct him.

The funeral doesn't take long to plan: Ma makes it similar to Dad's, ordering the same floral arrangements, the same prayer cards, the same music. Only the casket is different: Dad's was bronze, which best preserves the body. Eric's will be mahogany, a more economical choice. "It's all we can afford," Ma says.

Later, Loomis drives us through the cemetery to find a plot for Eric. We head to the north end, pull up at the bottom of a small hill where Dad is buried. But his grave is already surrounded, crowded with the more recent dead. "There," Ma says, walking uphill toward a small eucalyptus. She puts her hand on a low, thin branch, rubs a budding leaf between her fingers. "It's growing." She gives a quick survey of the area, decides this is the place.

"But your knee." I point out the steepness of the hill, warn her that years from now, when she's older, getting to Eric will be difficult.

"Then you help me," Ma says, starting toward the car. "You help me get to him."

BACK HOME, MA CALLS THE people we couldn't reach last night, and each conversation is the same: she greets them warmly, pauses, but can't catch herself before she gives in to tears. Meanwhile, I get the house ready, vacuuming upstairs and down, wiping dirty window screens with wet rags, rearranging furniture to accommodate the foot traffic of all the guests who will pray for my brother's soul. This will be the first of nine nights like this.

"I hate the way Filipinos die," Eric once said. It was the week of Dad's funeral. "Nine nights of praying on our knees, lousy Chinese food, and hundred-year-old women keep asking me where my girlfriend is." The businessmen were worse. On the last night of Dad's novena, one guy—he said he was related to us but couldn't explain how—tried selling life insurance to Eric and me. He quoted figures on what we could get for injury, dismemberment, death, and even took out a pocket calculator to prove how valuable our lives were. "Promise me, Edmond," Eric had said, "when I die, take one night to remember me. That's all. No old people. No kung pao chicken. No assholes telling you how much you'll get for my severed leg." He came close to crying, but then he managed a smile. "And make sure Village People is playing in the background."

"'YMCA'?"

"'Macho Man,'" he said. "Play it twice."

He started laughing. I started laughing. The house was full of mourners but we stood our ground in the corner of the room, matching in our Sears-bought two-piece suits, joking like the closest of brothers. But now I know we were wrong to talk like that, as though I would automatically outlive him. I was five years older than Eric, and he was only twenty-six.

Brothers are supposed to die in the correct order. I keep thinking: *Tonight should be for me.*

BY SIX, THE HOUSE FILLS with visitors. A dozen or so at first. Soon it's fifty. I stop counting at seventy-five.

Strangers keep telling me they're family. They try to simplify the intricate ways we're related: suddenly they're cousins, aunts and uncles, the godchildren of my grandparents. None of these people have seen Eric in years, have no idea of the ways he's changed. All they know about my brother is that he's dead.

Twice, an old woman calls me Eric by mistake.

When a neighbor asks, "Where's Delia?" Ma answers before I can. She's embarrassed by the idea of divorce, so she says that Delia is on the East Coast for business, but will be here as soon as possible. I wish it were true: I keep checking the door, thinking Delia might walk in any moment, that somehow she found out what happened and took the next flight out to be with me. Eric's death would have been our breakthrough, our turning point. I try not to think of tonight as a lost opportunity for Delia and me.

At seven, we get to our knees, pray before the religious shrine Ma's set up on top of the TV—a few porcelain figurines of Jesus Christ and the Virgin Mary, laminated prayer cards in wood frames, plastic rosaries. On the floor, an arm's reach from me, in front of the TV screen, stands an infant-sized ceramic statuette of Santo Niño, the baby Jesus Christ. All good Filipino Catholic families have one, but I haven't seen ours in years. He still looks weird to me, with his red velvet cape trimmed in gold thread and a crown to match, silver robes, brown corn silk hair curling down his face past his shoulders, the plastic flower in his hand.

When Eric was small, he thought Santo Niño was a girl: I caught him in his bedroom kneeling on the floor, and Santo

Niño was naked, his cape, robes, and crown in a small, neat pile by Eric's foot. For the first time, I saw how he was made: only the hands and face had been painted to look like skin; everywhere else was unglazed white, chipped in spots. "See," Eric said, his finger in the empty space between Santo Niño's legs, "he's a girl." I called him an idiot, tried to get it through his head that he was just a statue, a ceramic body that meant nothing. "Santo Niño is a boy," I said. "Say it." He wouldn't, so I took the Santo Niño from Eric, held him above my head. Eric jumped, reached, tried to get him back, knocked him out of my hands.

Ma heard the crash, ran upstairs and found pieces of Santo Niño scattered at our feet. Before she could speak I pointed at the pile of clothes on the floor, told her what Eric had done and said.

I tried putting Santo Niño back together in my room, and listened to Eric getting hit.

But my brother had a point. This second Santo Niño, the one Ma bought to replace the one we broke, does look like a girl, with glass-blue eyes, long black lashes, a red-lipped smile, offering a rose. When everyone's eyes are shut tight in prayer, I reach out, try to take it. It's glued to his fist.

WHAT STARTED AS PRAYING IS now a dinner party. Ma makes sure the egg rolls stay warm, that there's enough soy sauce in the chow mein. I hear her swap recent gossip with neighbors who moved away long before, watch her hold the babies of women who grew up on our street. In the Philippines, my parents threw three to four parties a year, and Ma boasted how her wedding was the grandest her province had ever seen. She promised equally grand weddings for us. But I was twenty-one when Delia and I eloped, and she gave up on Eric long ago. Funerals and novenas, I think, are all Ma has left.

People keep coming. I try to stay close to familiar faces: I comfort Mrs. Gonzalez, Eric's second-grade teacher, who's brought the crayon portraits Eric drew for her on paper sacks. I talk with Isaac Chavez, Eric's best friend from grade school and the first boy, Eric confessed to me later, he ever loved. He never told Isaac; maybe I should. But when Isaac introduces me to his new wife, I see no need to complicate his night.

Later, when the Mendoza brothers walk in, I stay away. A long time ago, at a Fourth of July picnic, they found Eric under the slide by himself, making daisy chains, singing love songs at the top of his lungs. I watched as they called him a girl, a sissy, a faggot. "That's what you get for playing with flowers," I told Eric later.

Ma catches me in the kitchen. "We're out of ice," she says. Beside her is a Filipino woman rattling melting ice cubes in her plastic cup. She looks like she came to dance instead of pray: her black hair falls in waves past her shoulders, and her tight black dress is cut above the knee. In her high-heeled boots, she's taller than almost everyone here.

"No problem." I take the cooler from the kitchen, step outside. The freezer is in the backyard, and its low hum is the only sign of life out here. The grass is weeds. Ma's roses are gone. And the four stalks of sugarcane Dad planted when he bought the house—one for each of us—have been dead sticks for years.

I take out a blue bag of ice, pound it against the concrete, breaking it up. Behind me the glass door slides open: it's the woman in the tight black dress. "This okay?" she asks. She means the cigarette between her fingers.

I slide the door shut. "It is now."

"I'm Raquel."

"Edmond." We shake hands.

"The brother." She lets go. "Cold."

Icy flakes stick to my fingers. I wipe them on my pants. "You're friends with Eric?"

"Sisters. That's what we call ourselves, anyway." She lights the cigarette, takes a drag, then lets out a long breath of smoke. "I have no family here. They're all back in Manila, pissed at me for leaving. So she became my sister. Sweet, huh?" *Sisters. She.* I feel like I'm being tested on what I know and don't know about my brother.

"Eric always wanted a sister."

"Well, if we're sisters, then that makes you my kuya Edmond, right?"

"Kuya?"

"That's Tagalog for 'big brother.'" Without asking, she unfolds a lawn chair and sits down. She crosses her legs, rests an elbow on her knee, her chin on her hand, looks at me closely. "How are you?"

Not even the coroner asked me that, even after I saw the body. "Fine." I squat down, smash more ice. "Holding up."

"Not me. Last night, when you left that message at the bar, I wanted to erase it. I was thinking, *I don't know anyone named Eric, and I don't know an Eric's brother*. But I knew who you meant."

She describes the rest of the night: how they closed the HoozHoo early, gathered the waitresses and the regulars together, drank and wept and sang songs until morning. Before everyone went home, they stood in a circle on the dance floor, held hands and said a prayer, music off but lights on, disco ball spinning above them. "It looked like heaven," she says. "All the girls wanted to come tonight, but I told them no. It should just be me. Out of respect for your mother."

It's like the start of a joke: *a dozen drag queens walk in on eighty Filipinos praying on their knees* . . . And I can picture the rest of it: six-foot-tall women in six-inch heels, glittering in a crowd of people dressed in black. I can see the stares, hear the whispers, Ma in the middle of it all, wishing them away. But maybe everyone would have been fooled, taken them as the very girlfriends that old ladies had pestered Eric about. Right away I knew what Raquel was, but so much of her looks real, like she was born into the body she's made.

"You're staring at my tits, hon."

The ice slips from my hand, slides across the cement onto the dirt.

She manages a smile, shrugs. "People look all the time."

She glances at them herself. "Four years ago, when I came to the States"—she gestures at her breasts, like she's trying to display them—"there's nothing here. Just flat. All empty. So now, if people want to look, I let them. They're mine, right?" She puts out her cigarette, lights another. "It's the same thing with Erica. Hers turned out really nice, really—"

"More ice?" I reach for another blue bag. "There's ice."

She reaches out, puts her hand on my shoulder. "I've embarrassed you. Sorry. That wasn't Coke in my cup." Raquel pulls a silver flask from her purse, unscrews the top, and holds it upside down. "All gone," she sighs. "I should be gone too." She gets up, but she's off balance. "Walk me to the door?" She puts her hands on my wrist, holds it tight. I don't know that I have a choice.

We step inside, work our way through the crowds in the kitchen, the living room. People look but they don't stare, and I think we can slip out quietly. But then I see the Mendoza brothers on the couch, eyeing Raquel, smirking at one another. My guess is that they've gone from childhood bullies to the kind of men who would follow a girl to her car with whistles and catcalls.

I help Raquel with her coat. "I'll walk you to your car."

"I'm at the end of the street." We step outside, walk down the driveway. Raquel takes my arm again, her hold tighter this time.

"Maybe you should've had Coke after all," I say.

"No," she says. "I need to be this way tonight."

We get to her car, a beat-up Honda dented all over, with

a missing back window replaced with plastic and duct tape. "Time for you to go back home," she says, leaning against the door. She searches her purse for her keys, not realizing she's holding them in her left hand.

Then she says, "Oh, shit."

I see it: on the corner, seven women, tall and big as Raquel, empty out of a minivan and head toward Ma's house, their heels clicking loudly against the sidewalk.

"I told them they shouldn't come," Raquel says. She takes a step toward them but I don't let her go. "It's not our problem," I say, then take the keys from between her fingers, walk her to the passenger's door. I unlock it for her, then get into the driver's seat.

"What about your guests?" Raquel asks.

"I don't have any." I start the car, watch the women enter Ma's house one by one. "Where to?"

"San Francisco."

I drive down Telegraph Avenue, head for the bridge.

"You're a nice man, Kuya Edmond." Raquel reclines her seat, turns toward the window, like she's watching the moon. "Can I call you that? Kuya?"

"Why not." No one else will, and Eric never did.

IT'S LESS THAN TEN MINUTES from Ma's house to the bridge, and yet I never cross it. Yesterday, when I drove to ID the body, was the first time in years that I'd been to San Francisco.

The time before that was when Ma kicked Eric out. He was seventeen. She found him in his bedroom, made up as a girl, in bed with a guy. She told them to leave, and told Eric not to come back. "For good this time," Eric said on the phone. "But there's nowhere for me to go." He was breathing fast and heavy, fighting not to cry.

Delia and I were living in Richmond, a good half hour away. But who else was going to help my brother? "Find a place," I said, "and I'll drive you there."

When I got to the house, Eric was sitting on the curb, a suitcase and an orange sleeping bag at his feet. He looked up at me, and what I thought were bruises was just makeup smeared together. "She tried wiping it off with a dishrag," he explained. "I look awful, don't I?"

"Get in the car," I said, then went inside to check on Ma. She was sitting at the top of the stairs, still in her Denny's uniform, Dad's terrycloth robe draped over her lap. She had just gotten home from a late shift when she found Eric. "I brought home a sandwich for him," she said. "He doesn't want to take it. If you're hungry—"

"I'm not," I said.

She nodded, went to her room. I heard her lock the door.

I went back outside, got in the car. Eric was in the passenger's seat, putting on lipstick. I grabbed his wrist, squeezed so hard he dropped it. "Didn't I tell you," I was shouting now, "you don't do this here. You want to play dress-up, that's fine. But not in Ma's house. You keep it to yourself."

"I'm not playing dress-up," Eric said.

I started driving. "Just tell me where to go."

Eric gave directions, and before I realized it I was on the Bay Bridge, bound for the city. He had a friend with a spare couch who lived in the Mission neighborhood. I headed down South Van Ness, turned onto a dark street that got darker the farther down we went. "Stop at the next house," Eric said. I pulled up in front of an old peeling Victorian. "Here," I said, and I put four twenty-dollar bills in his hand. He gave one of them back, reminded me that Mother's Day was coming up, and asked if I could get flowers for Ma.

He got out of the car, but before he closed the door he leaned in. "It was the first perfect night I ever had," he said. "Know what I mean?"

I didn't. "Call me in a few days," I said.

Eric walked toward the front door, dragging his things behind him. At the top of the driveway, he turned around. We looked at each other, as though neither of us knew who should be the first to go.

What I wished then I'm wishing now: that I'd reached over and opened the passenger door. Maybe then we could have made our way back to Ma's, or to a place neither of us had been to before. An all-night diner off the freeway. A road that dead-ended with a view of the city. If we'd had more time, I could have taken him home. Maybe then, things could have stayed the same.

It took me hours to find my way back to the bridge.

Ma finally spoke to Eric a year later, just in time for his

high school graduation. But she never invited him to live in the house again, and he never asked to come back. Eric's room is storage space now, but mine she left as is: my childhood bed against the window, my blue desk beside it, Dad's wicker rocking chair still in the corner. It's like she knew Eric was never coming back, and I always would.

I tap Raquel on her shoulder. "We're here," I say. "Tell me where to go."

FOR NOW, RAQUEL IS HOMELESS; a pipe burst in her apartment building three weeks before, flooding every unit. She'd been staying with Eric ever since. Had she said this before I got in her car, I'm not sure I would have driven her home.

It takes forty minutes to find parking, and when we do, it's blocks away from Eric's building. Walking, we pass drunken college boys negotiating with prostitutes, homeless kids sharing a bottle, cops who seem oblivious to everything around them. "I get scared at night," Raquel says. I let her keep hold of my arm.

Eric's building is on Polk Street. Two teenage girls sit on the front steps, smoking cigarettes. "New boyfriend, Miss Raquel?" one says.

"Ask me again in the morning and I'll tell you." Raquel laughs, high-fives both girls.

We take the stairs to the third floor, head down a narrow hallway lit by fading fluorescent lights. Eric's apartment number is 310. The door is white, like all the rest. "I'd meant to visit," I say. Raquel says nothing.

She takes the keys, lets me in. "After you, Kuya." I don't know how I'm getting home.

Those times I spoke to Eric, I imagined him sitting on his windowsill, and what his apartment might look like: wigs and dresses piled on a red leather couch, Christmas lights framing every window, drooping down from the ceiling. It was the kind of place where I would stand in the middle with my arms folded against my chest, careful not to touch anything; I'd keep an eye on the door, ready to escape at any moment. But when I step inside, everything is muted—there's a metal desk, a cream-colored futon, a cinderblock bookshelf with a stack of newspapers and magazines. On the windowsill are two framed pictures: one is of Ma and Dad in Long Beach, when they first came to the States, and the other is of me, from a time I don't remember. I'm just a kid, four or five, looking unbelievably happy. I don't know why or how. It seems impossible to me that anyone could be that pleased with life.

Raquel offers a tissue. I tell her I'm fine.

She goes into the tiny refrigerator beneath the desk, takes out a Mountain Dew and a small bottle of vodka. She mixes them in a paper cup, stirs it with her finger.

Then she takes out a bottle of pills from her purse.

"Headache?" I ask.

"Nothing's wrong with my head." She pops a pill in her mouth, sips her drink, makes a face when she swallows, like it hurts. "Hormones," she says, "no pain no gain." She takes another sip.

"There's pain."

"Figure of speech, Kuya. It goes down easy."

"There must be pain. There has to be." I think of Eric on a table, surgeons cutting into his body, needles vanishing into his skin. I think of that studio audience giving him the thumbs-down, like a jury deciding his fate. I think of Ma telling Eric he was dead. "The things you do. To prove yourself. We loved him as is. That should have been enough."

Raquel walks over, stands in front of me eye-to-eye. "You think that's why we do this? To prove a point to you? Listen, Kuya Edmond. All of this"—she unfolds her arms, takes my hand by the wrist and puts it on the center of her chest—"I did for me." She keeps it there, presses it into herself like I'm supposed to check for a heartbeat, but she lets me go before I can feel anything.

"I should get back," I say. She nods, walks me to the door. I make a tentative plan to stop by next week, to pick up some of Eric's things, though I'm not sure what I can rightfully claim. She says yes, of course, anytime, like she doesn't believe that I'll ever return here.

Just as I walk out the door, she hands me forty dollars for the cab ride back to Oakland, and refuses to take it back. "You brought me home," she says. "If you didn't, I could be dead too." She starts crying, then puts her hand on my face. I don't come closer, but I don't pull away either. "She loves you," she whispers, "okay?" Then she holds me, her body pressing against mine. I wonder if this is how Eric felt after he changed, if the new flesh made him feel closer to the person he held. I won't ever know, but I wish I could stay this way a little longer, listen to Raquel whisper about my brother the way she just did, in the present tense, like he's still going on.

THE NEXT MORNING, MA IS sitting at the bottom of the stairs, a vinyl garment bag over her lap. Eric's body is being prepared for tonight's viewing. We need to deliver his clothes.

She says nothing about the girls from the HoozHoo, doesn't ask me where I went. But on the way to the funeral home, I can feel her staring at me, like she's waiting for me to confess to something I didn't do.

Loomis is waiting in the lobby. "We've set up a room, Mrs. Dominguez," he says. We follow him through the lobby, but pass his office and continue down the hallway. "There's a phone inside, if you need anything." We stop in front of a metal door. He looks serious, like he's worried for us. "It's not too late to change your mind."

Ma shakes her head.

Loomis takes a breath, nods. "All right then." He turns to me. "It's good that you're here," he says, then leaves us.

Ma opens the door. I close it behind us. Eric lies on a metal table with wheels, a gray sheet covering him from the neck down. A strand of his hair hangs just over the edge, the darkest thing in this white room. I can see the incision on his neck, the thread keeping his lips shut.

Ma takes the garment bag from my hands. She goes to Eric. I stay by the door. "They have staff who can do this," I tell her.

She hangs the bag on a hook on the wall, unzips it. It's a suit. One of Dad's. "We have to change him." Ma puts her hand on Eric's right arm, rubs it up and down, the sheet still between them. She bends over, whispers *"Ang bunso ko"* between kisses to his cheek, his forehead, his cheek again, weeping. For a moment I mistake this for tenderness, her gesture of amends, a last chance to dress him the way she did when he was a boy.

Then she stands up straight, wipes her eyes, breathes in deep, and pulls several rolls of ACE bandages from her purse. Now I understand.

She lifts the sheet, folds it neatly down to his abdomen. For the first time, we see them, his breasts. They look cold and hard and dead as the rest of him, like they have always belonged to his body. If this was how he wanted to live, then this was how he wanted to die.

"Lift his arms," Ma says.

I don't move.

"This will work. I saw it on TV. Women who try to look like men. This is what they do."

"You can't."

"Everyone will see him tonight," Ma says, unrolling a bandage.

I tell her to forget tradition and custom, to keep the casket closed. "You picked out a nice casket for him. Beautiful flowers." I keep my voice calm and move toward her slowly, like a person trying to save someone from jumping off the ledge of a skyscraper. "They won't see," I say, "they won't know."

"I will," she says.

I reach for her arm but she pulls back. She steps around, stands behind Eric's head, slips her hands beneath his shoulders, manages to raise Eric a few inches from the table, but he slips from her. Ma tries again, her arms shaking from the weight of him, but she's just not strong enough. "Please," she says, looking at me. One way or another, she means to do this, and she'll only hurt herself in the end.

I walk over to the body. The light in here is different than it was in the morgue. Yesterday, the room seemed lit by a gray haze, and it took me only a second to recognize my brother. Today, the light makes shadows on his face, and I notice the sharpness of his cheekbones, the thin arch of his eyebrows. His lips are fuller than I remember, his neck more narrow. "It's still him," I say, but Ma doesn't believe me.

His body is hard from the embalming fluid, and he is heavier than I expected. To hold him up, I have to slip my arms beneath his, fold them across his chest. I can feel him, and I don't care how we look: we are together and we should stay this way, for all the moments we can. We have been apart for so long; soon he'll be gone for good. "Leave him alone," I say, but she doesn't listen, and then her hands separate me from my brother as she works the bandage round and round his breasts. I kiss the back of his neck, just once, in love and in apology.

Ma keeps going, another bandage and then one more, so tight the breasts vanish back into him, like they never existed. If my brother were alive, he wouldn't be able to breathe.

I SAY NOTHING TO MA on the way back to her house, and I let her off at the bottom of the driveway. Then I make my way to Telegraph Avenue, heading for the bridge.

I find my way to the Tenderloin, and as if it was meant to be, find a parking spot right in front of Eric's building. I hurry inside, pass the same two girls on the doorstep from last night, run up the three flights of stairs, down the hall to the end. I knock on the door.

"Who is it?" Raquel says.

"Edmond," I say. "The brother."

And she opens to me.

Felix Starro

WE WERE HERE TO PERFORM THE HOLY BLESSED
Extraction of Negativities on unwell Filipino Americans.
Mrs. Delgado was our 153rd patient, but we treated her
like the first and let her tell the story of her pain as if we
had never heard it before. "It begins here"—she tapped her
heart, then three spots on her stomach—"then here and
here, sometimes here. Bastard American doctors tell me
nothing is wrong, like I'm so old, so crazy-in-the-head."

"Then it's good you came to see us, ma'am," I said. I
helped her onto the massage table, laid her flat on her back.
Then I lit a pair of candles, hung plastic rosary beads over
the covered mirrors. A wreath of dried sampaguita flowers
made the cigarette air of our dingy hotel room smell like
Philippine countryside.

I unbuttoned her blouse halfway up, rubbed coconut
oil on her stomach, forehead, and chin. Then Papa Felix,
my grandfather, stepped forward. He rolled up his sleeves,
pulled his thinning hair into a ponytail. He put his palms

on Mrs. Delgado's belly and began to massage it, gently at first with his fingertips, then hard and deep with his fists. I closed my eyes, chanting Hail Marys over and over, faster and faster, and when I looked again Papa Felix's hands were half gone, knuckle-deep in Mrs. Delgado's body. Blood seeped out from between Papa Felix's fingers, and one by one he extracted coin-size fleshy blobs and dumped them into the trash can by his feet.

"Negativities," he said.

Mrs. Delgado lifted her head to look. "Thanks be to God," she said with a sigh I'd heard a thousand times before—that breath of relief that there is someone in the world, finally, who understands what hurts you.

There was a time when I might have apologized, if only in my head. "Two hundred dollars," I said. "Cash only."

I wiped the blood from her stomach, helped her to her feet. She reached for her purse, gave me the money. But then she did something no other patient had ever done before: she took out a camera. "When I told my sisters that Felix Starro was coming to San Francisco, they didn't believe me." She pressed a button, adjusting the zoom lens. "May I?"

Papa Felix shook his head: the camera flash could disrupt his spiritual vibrations, he said, which could thwart the healing of patients to come. "But for you," he said, "okay." He undid his ponytail, smoothed back his hair, and smiled. I moved to the right, to stand outside the picture.

· · ·

IN MY FAMILY, THE ONLY recipe passed down was the one for blood, but Papa Felix said I could never get it right. "Too thin," he said. "Like ketchup and water mix-mix." He dipped a finger into the plastic jug of blood and held it up to the fluorescent bathroom light. "What idiot would believe it's his own?"

Too much water, not enough corn syrup. Always my mistake. "At least it's red," I said, but he just grumbled about my carelessness and lazy attitude and insisted that something in America was making me different; he guessed it was the greasy food, the low-quality air of our hotel room, my terrible luck of turning nineteen in midair, en route from Manila to San Francisco. "I'm the same," I said, but he took my shoulders and stood me in front of him, flicked my temples twice and rubbed them in slow circles, as though what I was feeling could be diagnosed. "You're not right, Felix."

I was the third Felix Starro (my dead father was the second), and whenever Papa Felix said my name it meant he was serious; this time, I decided, he was just talking to himself. "You won't find anything," I said, and returned to the room. I took the rosaries and sheets off the mirrors, peeled away plastic crucifixes we'd taped to the walls, blew out the candles. I reached into hidden compartments underneath the massage table and carefully removed tiny plastic bags of blood, then dug through the trash to retrieve chicken livers good enough to use for the next day's Extractions.

Suddenly my cell phone vibrated in my pocket. I looked

up, checking to see that Papa Felix was still in the bathroom, then took it out. A text message read, *Buy roses. 6pm. 1525 South Van Ness.*

I left the livers where they were. I took the day's cash from the ice bucket, stuffed it into a manila envelope. "I'm going to the bank"—my voice shook, I could feel it—"to make the deposit." We'd found a Filipino bank near Chinatown where no one questioned large deposits of cash. I changed into a clean white shirt and my good corduroy pants, grabbed my backpack and Windbreaker from the closet.

"Look before you leave," he said. He meant that I should check the hallway, through the peephole, for anything suspicious; anyone, he said, could be undercover hotel security, ready to arrest us for our activities. But I didn't look, not this time, and I left the room so fast I nearly collided with a maid vacuuming the hall. She was a Filipina, plump-cheeked and short, younger than me. We had seen each other before.

"Excuse me," she said in English, "sorry," but I caught her staring at the DO NOT DISTURB sign on our doorknob. It was always there, to keep maids from finding the batches of blood and bags of chicken livers, or barging in on an Extraction. So the room was never cleaned, and though we kept it tidy ourselves, the Filipino housekeeper looked suspicious, as if thinking, *Dirty room.*

I said sorry, too, then walked slowly to the exit stairs, ran all the way down.

.   .   .

"DO YOU KNOW THIS PLACE, sir?" I showed the taxicab driver the address in the text message. He popped his gum and nodded, and we sped off before I could fasten my seat belt. In minutes I was far away from downtown. For the first time in America, I didn't know where I was.

We had arrived in San Francisco three weeks before. We worked seven days a week, up to ten hours each day, making the kind of money we could no longer make back home. Once, life was different: years before, Papa Felix had been one of the Philippines' top healers. He'd made his reputation by curing Batangas City mayor Agbayani's gout and action star B. J. San Remo's diabetes, which led him to becoming a regular Very Special Guest Star on *It's Real!! (Di Ba?)*, the paranormal TV variety hour that named the procedure the Holy Blessed Extraction of Negativities. Once a month for several years my grandfather, my father, and I made the two-and-a-half-hour drive from our home in Batangas City to the TV studio in Manila. I would sit in the last row of the live audience and watch Papa Felix in the monitors above, the zoom angles on his hands penetrating the patient's belly, like a ghost about to possess a body. When blood was shed the audience would gasp; when fleshy Negativities were extracted, they would cheer.

When I was ten, I snuck backstage to watch the performance. I hid behind the edge of a moveable wall, and as my father chanted Hail Marys into a microphone I saw Papa Felix slip a hand beneath the table and snatch something small and red—a bag of blood the size of a thumb. In an instant the Extraction began, and I felt a hand on the back of my neck. "You don't belong here," a stagehand said. He brought me to a white, windowless room, where I waited for what felt like hours, and when my father finally came I told him what I'd seen. He nodded slowly, stared at the ground. "Time to go home" was all he said. Two months later, he died in a jeep wreck, and at the post-funeral potluck I heard Papa Felix tell our guests I was his one comfort, a good, strong boy who would take his father's place: like a birth-mark, the family business was mine forever.

After some years, Mayor Agbayani's gout returned, followed by prostate cancer, and B. J. San Remo became a double amputee. The big-shot clients were gone, and our loyal following in nearby shantytowns brought in little money; I remembered long months when we were paid with eggs and sacks of rice. "Even the peasants are rip-ping us off," Papa Felix griped. And then two years ago, his old rival Chitz Gomez began performing surgeries on Filipinos abroad in Guam and Saudi Arabia, and returned a far wealthier man than before. "We can do better," Papa Felix said. He called on old connections to help him build a client list in California, then scheduled our trip to San Francisco, where there were plenty of Filipinos in need of healing. It was true: our first patient, a middle-aged sales clerk with stomach tumors and a fear of doctors, fell to his knees when he stepped into our hotel room. "You're here," he said, taking Papa Felix's hand and pressing it against his forehead, "finally." It was amazing that there were people who remembered Felix Starro—and even more amazing that they still believed in him.

At the end of our first week Papa Felix said, "How I pity them, these Filipinos in America. So many sick without knowing why." He was standing at the hotel window looking down at the crowds in the street, as if they were his people. "Can you imagine, waiting and waiting, just for someone to bring you hope?"

I lied and said no.

"BUY ROSES" WAS A CODE from a woman named Flora Ramirez; 1525 South Van Ness was the address of her flower shop, which was squeezed between a Mexican bakery and a liquor store. On the storefront window, yellow curly letters spelled out BUHAY BULAKLAK, which translated strangely from Tagalog—it meant "life flowers" in English. I took a deep breath, but just as I reached for the doorknob I glimpsed a streak of dried blood over the ridge of my knuckles. I licked my thumb and rubbed it away, checked my other hand. It was clean. I went inside.

The store was barely bigger than our hotel room, lined with flower-filled shelves and humming refrigerators; everywhere you moved, it seemed, flowers would touch you. A woman was standing at a wooden table behind the cash register. She had a pair of scissors in one hand, white flowers in the other, and one by one she snipped them in half, letting stems fall to the floor. She was not tall, but her tailored blazer and the tight bun of her hair made her seem like a serious businessperson, someone who could get things done. Though I had never seen Flora Ramirez's picture, I knew it was her. It had to be.

She greeted me in English, like I was any ordinary American customer. I meant to identify myself but was unsure if it was safe to speak: there was one other customer, an old, bent-over woman in a dirty ski jacket with a scarf on her head, moving from bouquet to bouquet, rubbing petals between her fingers.

Flora Ramirez looked at me and said, "You want to buy roses."

I nodded.

"Roses are on sale. Seven for seven dollars. Red, pink, yellow, white. What is your preference?" She put down her scissors, stepped around the register, and slid open the refrigerator door. Cold, rose-scented air floated toward me, and suddenly I feared her text message was no code at all, that our meeting truly was about flowers and nothing else.

"Red, pink, yellow, white," she said again.

"Yellow," I said.

"Yellow means friendship." She took seven yellow roses from the refrigerator and carried them to the register. She wrapped them in cellophane and rung them up, then hand-wrote a bill on a small pad of paper. She tore it off, handed it to me. It said *$25000*—the initial payment.

"Everything is fine." She smiled, and something about her perfect teeth let me know that I was right to seek her out.

For twenty-five thousand dollars, Flora Ramirez could help illegal Filipinos stay in America—months or years, forever if they wished. I didn't know how she did it, only that she could: two years before, she had given TonyBoy Llamas, my girlfriend Charma's favorite cousin, a new life. He was vacationing in California before returning to the Philippines to join the seminary when he met and fell in love with an amateur Mexican boxer. His parents disowned him, his brothers, too, so he and the boxer sought help from Flora Ramirez. Six months later, they were living in what TonyBoy called a Mediterranean-style apartment complex in Las Vegas, earning good money dealing blackjack. So when Papa Felix began planning our trip to America, I knew this would be my chance: I made contact with Flora Ramirez and started a yearlong correspondence of coded e-mails and text messages, coordinating cash amounts and payment dates and when, where, and how we would meet. These were risky, secret dealings, but in times of doubt Charma would tell me, "If my homosexual priest cousin and his Mexican boxer boyfriend can make it in America, why can't we?" We were no different from them, she said, or any other person in search of a good and honest life.

Flora Ramirez tapped her fingernail twice on the receipt. I unzipped my backpack, took out the envelope of cash, handed it to her. She slipped it underneath the register drawer, then tied a black ribbon around the bouquet of roses. "Better selection tomorrow," she said, "you come back then. Same price." She nodded toward the door.

I left the store and walked to the corner to hail a taxicab. My heart was pounding; people on the street stared at me, as if they knew who I was and what I'd done. But it was merely the roses in my hands that caught their attention. They were lovely and bright; I could imagine pressing them between the pages of a heavy book, a souvenir that would inspire me to look back on this day, the first of my new life. But for now they would only make Papa Felix suspicious, so I left them on top of a trash can for someone else to take.

WHENEVER I CALLED CHARMA, I'D stare at postcards of famous San Francisco landmarks, images of which she would download online—the Golden Gate Bridge, Coit Tower, the famous crooked street. It was like taking in the same view together, despite the distance between us, and she'd say the pictures were glimpses of our future. But now, I was calling from the backseat of a dented, lime-green cab, staring at a lightning-shaped crack in the window.

She picked up on the fourth ring. "I bought roses," I said.

First she giggled, then she gasped. "You really did it? Truly?"

"First payment was today. Second tomorrow. And then—"

"Pay it all now!" she said. "Pay it all now and send me a plane ticket tomorrow and let's be together forever."

"That's not how it works. Flora Ramirez has a process."

I reminded Charma that it might be months, maybe longer, until I could send for her; though Flora Ramirez had connections with people who could help find me work and a place to sleep, it would take time to begin a life. "Have faith," I said.

"Always. What about the old man?"

"He doesn't know anything. And once I get my papers, there's nothing he can do."

Then she said, "How will you go?"

There was static, silence, then an awkward moment when I caught the driver's eyes in the rearview mirror. He seemed dubious, though I was speaking Tagalog. "Are you there?" Charma said, but I had no answer, not yet, despite the exit scenarios playing in my head: I imagined going to the airport with Papa Felix, then backing away into the crowds as soon as he crossed through security. Or I would take my seat on our return flight and then, minutes before takeoff, tell Papa Felix I'd forgotten something in the terminal bathroom, and make my escape from there. Sometimes I didn't even imagine the airport; I simply left in the middle of the night.

"How will you go?" Charma repeated.

"I'll leave a note," I finally said, a good enough answer for now.

BACK AT THE HOTEL, PAPA Felix was sitting on a chair in the bathroom staring at the mirror, a paper cup in his hands and a bottle of Cutty Sark by his feet. "You forgot me," he said. "I've been waiting." He was wearing a white trash bag like a poncho, and a box of hair dye was on the edge of the sink. At home, I colored his hair twice a month; here, once a week. "A good healer should look ageless," he always said, "like Jesus or Dick Clark."

I hung my windbreaker and backpack in the closet, stepped into the bathroom. "Long lines at the bank."

"Cut in line next time. Receipt?"

From my pocket I pulled out an ATM receipt I'd found on the sidewalk a week before. He squinted at the small paper, as though his old eyes could actually make out the tiny numbers. "Good work, good money," he said. "And just think: What did we come with? Nothing. Now look at us." He finished his whiskey, poured another. "Maybe we'll come back another year. New York next time. Maybe Canada. Where are the Filipinos in Canada?" He named other countries and continents we might visit; the way he talked, the whole planet was full of ailing Filipinos far from home, waiting for us to heal them.

"Someday," I said, "maybe." In the mirror, there was an odd, faraway look in Papa Felix's eyes, like he was trying to remember something long forgotten. I realized he was watching me. I reached for the box of dye and tore it open, pulled out the bottle and latex gloves, and I found him still watching, like he was studying my face for a twitch or new expression I'd adopted, some clue to who I really was and what I was planning to do.

"When we're home," he finally said, "you're on your own."

"My own." I didn't understand.

"You're nineteen now. A man. Your father was sixteen when he first extracted on his own. It's your time." He emptied and refilled his drink, then set a paper cup on the counter and poured one for me. "Two of us working, side by side. Double Felix Starro, double business." He lifted his cup, toasting a future that would never happen.

There was only one thing to do. I took the whiskey, drank it in a single gulp. I felt its warmth, then its sting.

He nodded, drank his whiskey, poured another. He settled back in his chair and looked at his reflection almost admiringly, then pointed to his roots. "All this silver," he said, "make it black."

FOUR CUPS OF WHISKEY MADE Papa Felix drowsy. I poured a fifth that put him to sleep. It was barely eight o'clock when I tucked him into bed, but he snored thunderously—someone from the next room pounded on the wall, as if that could quiet him down. "Are you awake?" I whispered. I crossed the room and spoke again. "Can you hear me? Wake up!" But his snoring only grew louder, and I knew it was safe.

I went into the closet, unlocked my suitcase and opened it, unzipped the lining. The money was there, paper-clipped in flimsy stacks. It was almost a disappointment, how little twenty-five thousand American dollars could look; it seemed mathematically impossible that so small an amount could guarantee my next life. But back home, it could keep a family stable for several generations, or get an entire village through a difficult year. Half asleep on the plane from home to here, I'd dreamed that I'd refunded every person Papa Felix had ever touched; in that same dream my father told me, *Go, go*.

I took two stacks of cash and put them in my backpack for my second visit to Flora Ramirez. I locked my suitcase, closed the closet.

I went into the bathroom to prepare for the next day. I made the blood first—I poured corn syrup into a plastic jug, mixed in water, then thirty drops of red dye. But the lid to the jug was missing, so instead of shaking the jug to make the mix, I rolled up my sleeve and stirred it with my hand. Long ago, Papa Felix made it the same way; because my hands were small, my job was to squirt the liquid into tiny bags and knot them up. We'd stay up all night, diligent and silent, as though our work was truly blessed and holy.

I finished making the bags of blood and liver, tied them shut and stashed them in the foam cooler beneath the sink. There were streaks of blood along the counter and faucet, red fingerprints on the doorknob and toilet seat. Our nightly crime scene, but not for long, not for me. I cleaned up fast, then showered, and under near-scalding water I scratched dried blood from my wrists and fingers, the backs of my hands, my knuckles and the skin in between.

Back in the room, Papa Felix was still snoring. I walked over, sat on the edge of my bed, an arm's reach away. The Cutty Sark was on the nightstand, so I unscrewed the cap and drank from the bottle, thinking of the note I told Charma I'd leave behind, all the things that could be said—a quick apology maybe, the hope he would understand, a promise that we would both be okay. The more I drank, the more the note went on—it would have been pages, had I truly written it. But then the pounding on the wall started again, so I pounded back and told whoever it was to let my grandfather sleep.

WE PERFORMED TWELVE EXTRACTIONS THE next day. Most who came were elderly, complaining of arthritis, swollen joints, unending fatigue. But the last patient, a woman named Maribel, was just thirty-two years old. She'd come with her little boy, who sat on a pillow in the corner. Despite his video game, he watched us the whole time, the fear plain on his round face.

After, as Maribel got to her feet and buttoned up her blouse, I noticed that her right breast was gone. She caught me looking. "If only you'd come sooner," she said, blinking back tears. She gave me the money, and I took it.

"I'm sorry," I said, and then I heard giggling. I turned and saw Papa Felix sitting on the edge of his bed, entertaining the boy with a vanishing coin trick. He'd done the same with me when I was that age, making random objects disappear and reappear in his hands—a spool of thread, a mango pit, even a newborn chick. Then he would say, "Tell me how I did that," his voice heavy and grave, as though sleight of hand could save a life instead of deceive one. But I couldn't explain it; all I could think about was the time and space between the vanish and return, where a small thing went in its moment of absence—I pictured some dead, barren planet without weather or sound, and I'd lie awake at night, determined not to dream of it.

I took the boy's hand, pulled him gently toward his mother, and saw them out. Then I gathered the day's cash, grabbed my things. Papa Felix was about to say something—I heard him call my name—but I left without saying goodbye: it was the best way, I decided, to go.

I ARRIVED AT BUHAY BULAKLAK at 6 P.M. exactly. I was about to step in when a family stepped out, a Filipino couple and their baby. They looked tremendously pleased; even the baby seemed to smile. I moved aside to let them pass, watched them until they turned the corner.

Inside, Flora Ramirez was alone. She was sitting at the table behind the cash register, a thick, long-stemmed tropical flower in each hand, staring at a vase. "Birds-of-paradise," she said. "Beautiful, eh?" I nodded, but I felt anxious, thinking about the family I saw and the ways she might have helped them.

"I have the money." I could feel my heart speeding up. "I want to stay here and I have the money."

She put down her flowers. She pulled a wooden stool from beneath the table and told me to sit. I joined her at the table, handed her the envelope of cash. She slipped it into the pocket of her blazer without counting it.

She reviewed the terms of our agreement, the obligations met so far. I'd made the first two payments ("Nonrefundable," she said, in both English and Tagalog) and would bring the remaining twenty thousand dollars two days from now, plus an extra thousand to cover unexpected costs. This would guarantee a California ID, a Social Security card, various documents like school diplomas, recent utility bills, a birth certificate. "What you need to start a life. And you're ready for it? If not, you're wasting my time." She was speaking Tagalog now, her voice louder than before. "Like the old people who come to me," she said. "They want to stay, to be with their children, collect Social Security. Then what: they're suddenly scared to spend their last years away from home. They say, 'We are old, we cannot die away from home, blah blah blah.' What's wrong with dying here? The cemeteries aren't good enough?" She reached into a pile of random flowers, grabbed a handful and jammed them into the vase. "In the end, your land is just the dirt you're buried in."

I looked at Flora Ramirez. "I don't care where I'm buried," I said.

She stared at me for a moment, and I knew she believed me.

"You need a picture," she said. She got up from her stool

and stepped into a tiny office, pointed at a bare, blue wall, and had me stand against it. Then she reached into her desk for a digital camera and told me to be still.

She took my picture. "Why did you come?"

She had never asked the question before. Our months of correspondence were all business; she'd needed to know only my age and gender.

"For a happy life." That was my answer.

She took a second picture, then the last. "Then it's good you came to me."

We stepped out of the office. We arranged to meet two days later, this time at her home. On the back of a business card she wrote *La Playa @ Lincoln*, but not her actual address. "Count seventeen houses down," she said. "I live there." Then she took some flowers, wrapped them in cellophane, tied them with black ribbon.

I thanked her, exited the shop. People on the street seemed to watch me again; I told myself it was the flowers. But sweat was dripping down my neck, soaking my collar, and my heart was beating so fast I swore I could hear it—if Felix Starro powers were real, I would have reached inside myself and pulled it out.

ON THE RIDE BACK TO the hotel, I couldn't get hold of Charma. My signal faded in and out, even stuck in traffic. A text message that said *ALL PERFECT* was the best I could do.

The driver let me off two blocks from the hotel. I walked the rest of the way, and when I crossed the street I spotted the Filipino maid sitting at a crowded bus stop. I didn't intend eye contact, but it was the first time in America that I knew a face among the hundreds of strangers I passed every day.

She smiled meekly. "Beautiful flowers," she said.

I'd almost forgotten the bouquet in my hand—I'd meant to leave them on a trash can again—so I offered them to her, but she was shy to accept. "They'll die in that room," I said.

She took the bouquet, sniffed the single rose.

Then she grabbed my hand. "Your grandfather," she said, "he helps people?" She'd noticed all our come-and-go visitors, how despondent they looked when they arrived, how peaceful when they left. "I have money. I can pay." I told her she was mistaking us for other people, but she said there was no need for me to lie. "I know he can help me," she whispered in Tagalog. "I know who Felix Starro is." Her grip tightened, her thumb pressing on my inner wrist like she was desperate to find a pulse.

"Stay away from him," I said. I stepped back, slipped into the crowd, and hurried off.

In the hotel room, I found Papa Felix staring out the window. "You were talking to the maid."

I locked the door behind me. "You were watching me?"

"Does she know who we are?" I told him no, but he rambled on with paranoid scenarios of the police discovering us, confiscating our client list, robbing us of our hard-earned money. "One mistake and we're finished."

"She was just talking about home," I said, and made up a story about distant relatives she had in Batangas City, former teachers at my old elementary school. Then I poured him a cup of Cutty Sark and assured him once more: "She doesn't know anything."

"She'd better not. Because if she does, and if she talks, then our time here means nothing." He picked up the fading, wrinkled ATM receipt and held it to my face. "This is our future. Don't forget that."

I gave him the whiskey and stepped toward the window, looked down at the street. The bus stop was at least two long blocks west of the hotel—I had to press against the glass just to see it. From where I was, the people standing there were faceless, blurry bodies. How Papa Felix could spot me with his old, bad eyes was beyond me, and a familiar feeling returned: that he possessed a real kind of power after all, some extra sense that could lead him to me, wherever I was.

HE WAS STANDING OVER ME when I woke the next morning. "I'm going with you," he said.

He meant the butcher shop in Chinatown. The chicken livers I bought were too fresh, he said, therefore fake-looking. With one day left, there was no time for my mistakes.

He set a Snickers bar and a banana next to my pillow. "Eat breakfast and let's go."

On my own, the walk to Chinatown took seventeen minutes; with Papa Felix, it was twice as long. But I stayed ahead, by half a block sometimes, and when he caught up at the butcher shop he was out of breath, and he accused me of trying to lose him in the crowd. He took a seat on a bench outside the Chinese bakery next door, then gave me a fifty-dollar bill. "Just get it done," he said.

I entered the shop, pushed my way through the crowd to take a number. They called me twenty minutes later; I paid for the livers and left. But outside, the bench was empty; Papa Felix was inside the bakery now, sitting at a corner table with three silver-haired Chinese women. They leaned in as he spoke, nodding despite the quizzical looks on their faces. I couldn't remember the last time he'd solicited business like this, but his method was the same—he tapped their foreheads with his thumb, shut his eyes, and mouthed secret prayers to himself. It was always a bogus-looking act, but at some point I just assumed that Filipinos were somehow predisposed to believing anyone who claimed to understand their pain. And yet I could imagine these Chinese women making appointments with Papa Felix, who would insist they pay up front, then arrange for them to meet us long after we'd gone; he'd done it before. I pictured these women knocking on our hotel door, awaiting help that would never come.

I went inside, walked up to Papa Felix. "I'm ready to go," I said. His eyes were still closed and he kept on praying, so I shook his shoulder. "Open your eyes. Let's go."

He turned to me, gave a mean look that I gave right back. "I'm *working*," he said.

"I'm not." I slammed the bag of livers on the table. The Chinese women glared at me with scolding faces.

I walked to the end of the block. I tried to cross, but the light was red, and Papa Felix caught up with me. "What were you trying to do in there?" he asked.

I pressed the button for the crosswalk. "Nothing."

"The maid yesterday. Those women today. You're trying to tell them about us?"

I pressed the button again and again.

"You think I'm stupid." He grabbed my arm, squeezed it tight. "I know about you, Felix."

He was stronger than I thought. "Let me go," I said, then finally pushed him off. He stumbled back, almost fell, and the bag of livers slipped from his hands, everything inside spilling onto the sidewalk.

The traffic light was still red, but I crossed the street. Papa Felix would be close behind me, so I walked faster, zigzagging through the tourist crowds. Police blocked the next intersection—a moving truck had rear-ended a minivan—and I couldn't continue. So I turned around, ready to face him, to say whatever needed to be said. But he wasn't there. I started back through the crowds and finally found him still on the corner, head bowed like a mourner at a grave. He was bent down, picking up the livers from the sidewalk, one by one; a true believer might have thought he was extracting Negativities from the Earth itself. To me, he looked like a penniless man gathering coins.

"Just leave them," I said. "Let's go." Standing over him, I could see the silver in his roots, all that I'd missed.

What else could I do? I joined Papa Felix on the ground and helped him clean up. People who passed us looked curious, then repulsed by the livers in our hands. Some shook their heads, like they couldn't believe what they were seeing.

THAT WHOLE DAY HIS FOCUS was off. Twice he palmed a liver but not a blood bag, which made for oddly bloodless Extractions. Then he did the opposite with the last patient, extracting nothing but blood. He tried to explain: "Nothing is there. Nothing is wrong with you." The patient got up and refused to pay, then peeled a plastic crucifix from the wall and dropped it on the ground. He slammed the door on his way out, so hard the walls shook. And I realized I was done.

I began cleaning up, one last time, and made no ceremony of it: I simply put things away. All the while Papa Felix just stood by the window, staring straight ahead at the vacant building across the street. Only when I took the day's cash from the ice bucket did he finally speak. "Don't deposit the money," he said. "You keep it. Belated birthday gift."

Birthday. I had turned nineteen three weeks before, on the plane to America. But I didn't know exactly when it happened—that whole time in the sky I wasn't sure if it was today or tomorrow, which country was ahead or behind and by how many hours or days—not until Papa Felix leaned over, in the moment before he fell asleep, to whisper, "Happy Birthday."

I put the cash in my pocket. "I'll take it to the bank."

"I know what you think of me, Felix. But it's the best I could do." He was still staring out the window, but squinting now, as if the evening moon were unbearably bright. "Can you tell me the name of a man who would do any different?"

I didn't answer. I grabbed my windbreaker and backpack. I checked the peephole before leaving, but as I stepped into the hall I noticed a small, white envelope on the floor. I picked it up. Inside was a picture of Papa Felix, and on the back was a note that read *Felix Starro and Felix Starro. Regards, Mrs. Celica Delgado*. It was the photo she'd taken two days before, and when I looked closer I saw part of me within it, the very edge of my face. But what struck me was Papa Felix's graying eyes and the sinking skin beneath, his knobby shoulders, the fading color of his old hands.

THAT NIGHT, PAPA FELIX SLEPT even more deeply, and I took the cash from the inner lining in my luggage and packed it into a large, padded envelope, then put it inside my backpack. I slipped into bed but stayed awake. It was morning by the time I finally closed my eyes, noon when I woke.

Papa Felix was dressed, packing his clothes. "Last full day in America," he said.

I got out of bed. "You didn't wake me."

"It's a long plane ride back," he said. "Best to sleep now, as much as you can."

I showered, dressed. My meeting with Flora Ramirez was at 3 P.M.; I told Papa Felix I would spend the day souvenir shopping. "Souvenirs," he said. "Waste of money, waste of time. What's to remember about this place?" He looked at me expectantly, as though he wouldn't move or speak until I answered.

I gathered my things, promised to be back before dark.

THE TAXICAB DRIVER SAID THAT Flora Ramirez lived on the edge of the continent. "If the big one hits," he said, "you're out to sea."

We turned onto La Playa, stopped in front of the seventeenth house. Metal bars covered the windows, and dried-up ivy spread over the walls, hiding the address.

I stepped out of the cab, walked to the door. I meant to knock but she opened first, as though she'd been watching me through the peephole. I followed her in, up a flight of carpeted stairs to the living room. This was my first time in an American house, but it wasn't so different from any house back home—there was a two-person couch and a white wicker rocking chair, a small glass table in between. I'd expected flowers, but there were none that I could see, not even a vase.

The house was silent, and I wondered if Flora Ramirez had any family. Yet on the floor, propped against the wall, was a large picture frame full of faces and bodies cut out from photos, like a creature with a hundred different heads. Closer, I saw that they were all Filipino, some smiling, some not, and I recognized one of them, a small body in the middle. It was TonyBoy, Charma's cousin. His hand was up like he was waving hello or goodbye at the camera. I wondered when my picture would be added, where Flora Ramirez would place it.

"Those are the ones I help," Flora Ramirez said. There were several brown envelopes in her hand. "Do you see how happy they are?"

"I see TonyBoy." I pointed at his picture.

She blinked.

"TonyBoy Llamas. My girlfriend's cousin."

She nodded, then put the envelopes on the table. "Check them." She sat on the rocking chair.

I picked one up, took out the ID card inside. It was a driver's license, my first ever; blue capital letters spelled out CALIFORNIA across the top. My picture was grainy and faded, as if taken years instead of two days before, and the expression on my face surprised me, how it matched what I felt now: my eyes were focused but blank, my mouth plain and straight as a minus sign.

Then I saw it.

John Arroyo Cruz was the name printed beside my face. The signature below spelled it out, unmistakably.

"Is there a problem?" Flora Ramirez asked.

"John," I said.

"Nobody keeps a name. That's not the process."

I set the card down on the table.

She said it again: "Nobody keeps a name."

The thing to do was nod and say, *I understand,* to accept what she had done with gratitude, without questions. But I wanted to know: "Who is he?"

She leaned back in the rocking chair, silent for a moment, like she didn't want to answer. "A store clerk from L.A.," she finally said. "Killed one year ago. I know the parents." I glanced over the faces on the floor. I wondered what names Flora Ramirez had given them, and what people she had taken them from.

Suddenly my cell phone vibrated in my pocket. It was Charma. "I need to answer," I said. "Sorry."

She got up from her chair, said, "Be quick," then went into the kitchen.

I flipped open my phone, moved to the corner of the room. "I can't talk," I whispered, "but listen: How's Tony-Boy?"

"Who?" Static crackled over Charma's voice. "Are you there?"

"I'm here. Have you heard from TonyBoy?"

"TonyBoy?" She paused. "Not in months. Maybe a year. Why?"

I looked out the window. Beyond the metal bars the ocean appeared motionless, the clouds above equally still, and on the street below there was no one, just a few cars passing by. At the end of Flora Ramirez's driveway, a trash can lay on its side, rolling back and forth with the wind. I imagined myself in the future, walking down a similar street: If someone called out *John*, would I answer? Would I even turn around?

I told Charma I had to go, then hung up without saying goodbye.

Flora Ramirez returned, sat in her rocking chair. I took my place on the couch. She mentioned the hour, the other appointments she had today, and I knew it was time for me to pay. I unzipped my backpack. The padded envelope was right there, plump with all the cash inside, but I pretended to search through the various compartments of my bag. "I made a mistake," I said. I explained I had two similar bags, one for sightseeing and one for business, and I'd brought the wrong one with me. "If I could have more time"—I zipped up my backpack—"I can bring it later today."

She stared at me for a moment; I knew she didn't believe me. But she didn't call me a liar, didn't reach for my backpack. She simply rocked back and forth, like she was giving me a chance to confess the truth. "If I could have more time," I said again, and my heart would not slow down.

"You do what you need to do." She looked out the window, toward the ocean.

"I'm sorry," I said.

We stood up, and I followed her down the stairs. Neither of us mentioned my possible return, and neither of us said goodbye. I wondered if Flora Ramirez was her real name, and if not, who she had been before.

I walked to the end of the block and waited for a taxicab, remembering the driver's license and the life I'd glimpsed from it: John Arroyo Cruz lived in a city called Riverside, was born two years before I was. His eyes were brown—mine were true black—and he was five feet six inches, slightly shorter than me. At the bottom of the license, I had noticed the word *donor*, and now I pictured myself dead, thinking, if I were not Felix Starro anymore, what would be taken from me, what would be left.

DESPITE MY STEADY CELL PHONE signal on the taxi ride back, I didn't call Charma. Instead, I typed a text message that said *There is a problem*. What it meant exactly, I didn't know; but as I hit SEND, the days ahead became perfectly clear: there would be sixteen hours on a plane, sitting across the aisle from Papa Felix, yet in the moments before landing I would wish for takeoff again, just a little more time in midair. Then, it would be night after night of jet lag, sitting on the edge of my bed, wide awake.

It was almost dark by the time I returned to the hotel. I took the elevator up, and when the door slid open the Filipino maid was standing there, purse clutched to her chest. I stepped out and she stepped in. Her eyes were red from crying, but she couldn't stop smiling; and just as the door slid closed I heard it again—a sigh, that breath of relief.

I ran to Papa Felix.

The room smelled like sampaguitas again, and everything was back—the massage table, the rosaries and crucifixes, the candles. Papa Felix was at the bathroom sink, scrubbing his hands. "Was she here?" I said. "The maid?"

He looked at me in the mirror. "Liar," he said. "That girl knew all about us."

"What did you do to her?"

"I helped her. That girl is pregnant. And do you know why she came to see me? To take it out of her. She said it was a miracle that I was here to fix it." He dried his hands, then reached beneath the sink for the Cutty Sark. "Sixteen, pregnant, wanting to kill her baby. It's an ugly country."

"She thinks it's gone? That everything is okay?"

"I helped that girl, more than she knows. Someday she'll understand. You, too, God willing." He poured what was left of the whiskey, drank it down. I imagined the maid walking along the street with peace of mind, dazzled by the miracles of Felix Starro, so grateful for them. I thought how light she must feel, believing all her Negativities were gone, just like that.

"I have to go," I said.

I walked out of the room, hurried down the back stairs, left the hotel, ran two blocks. The maid was sitting at the bus stop, purse still clutched to her chest, and I could see her bus slowly approaching. I grabbed her wrist. "Take this," I said, then reached into my backpack, into the envelope, and removed a handful of cash. She looked confused, almost frightened of me, but I told her she would need it, and I put the wad of bills in her hands. Then in Tagalog I whispered, "Everything you believed was wrong."

The bus came. I let her go and backed away, then started toward the hotel, wondering how much money I'd given her, how much I'd be short. I imagined Flora Ramirez sitting in her chair, staring at me as she rocked back and forth. I would apologize for lying, then confess that I didn't have all the money but swear to pay the rest soon. And despite my speeding heart, I would smile and breathe calmly, to prove that I was ready for whatever name she could give me.

I stepped to the curb and raised my hand to hail a taxicab. High above, I thought I saw Papa Felix in the window, looking down and waving hello, as though I were waving, too.

The View from Culion

ROBED IN WHITE, SISTER MARGUERITE APPEARS AT my door like a ghost. She smiles, and a crack in her lower lip widens.

"Blood," I tell her, pointing to my lip, "right there." She wipes away the red dot with her thumb. She doesn't worry, knows it's just the heat of Culion that has dried her skin.

She enters my room and sits beside me on the edge of my bed. Without asking, she takes the sketchbook from my lap and looks at a drawing of a piece of driftwood on my windowsill, and the lace curtain behind it. Most days I'd sketch something outside—the church doors, the Spanish tile roof of the hospital, the palm trees that tower over the colony—but the afternoon is too warm, too bright.

"It's a lovely picture," she says.

I take back the book and close it. "It isn't finished."

She pats my knee, then sets a small burlap bag filled with oranges between us. I haven't seen an orange in years, though the doctors who live just outside the colony supposedly buy them from the occasional merchant boat. "For the American," she says. "You'll bring this to him?"

I set the bag by my feet. "If I have to."

The American, a soldier gone AWOL from the U.S. Navy, arrived three days ago. He was collected from a church-run leprosarium just outside Manila, delirious with fever and covered with lesions and sores. The fever has broken, but he refuses to cooperate with the doctors, and demands to be returned to the Philippines. "But to what kind of life?" she says. "Who would have him? He can't go back to the Navy. They would punish him, leaving the way he did."

"If he's a deserter," I say, "maybe he should be punished."

"He is with us now. He doesn't have a choice."

A moth crawls along the window. I flick it through a tear in the screen. "But why me? Let someone else speak to him."

"It's best that an American speak to him. Someone who can understand what he's going through."

"I'm not an American."

"You know what I mean."

Warm wind blows through the room; the curtain rises, falls. "I'll bring him the oranges, whatever else you want. But after this, no more visits." I get up and take a rubber band from my dresser, pull back my hair into a ponytail. Sister Marguerite offers to comb it for me, but I tell her I can manage on my own. "When you were a girl," she says, "you would let me." Except for the doctors and nurses,

Sister Marguerite was the first person to touch me after I arrived on Culion.

I give her the rubber band, the comb. She takes my hair into her hands and I close my eyes, feel the teeth of the comb slide gently against my scalp. "The only place for him is here," she says. "He needs to understand this." When she finishes, she turns me around to face her, like she is checking to make sure I'm presentable.

"Then that's what I'll tell him."

She leaves my room, shuts the door behind her. I take my sketchbook and draw the gnarled, twisty ends of the driftwood, the lace curtain, another moth on the sill.

AT HIS INSISTENCE—AND TO THE relief of the hospital staff—the American has been given his own quarters away from the other patients, in an old concrete shack atop the hill behind the church. In my time in the colony, no one has ever lived in it, and over the years children have passed along the rumor that it houses the fallen limbs of dead patients. Once, I heard a boy with a missing eye and atrophied fingers ask a nurse if this was true. The nurse laughed and told him no, that the room was nothing but dust and air.

I make my way there now.

The day feels hotter than before, but everyone is out in the colony plaza, clustered together wherever there's shade. Old women sit beneath the post office awning, weaving crude baskets from dried banana leaves. A group of men smoke cigarettes in the shadow cast by a gutted wartime bus. It's the younger ones who brave the sun, playing made-up games with shells and stones around the dried-up fountain. I was their age when I arrived in 1954, barely ten years old, but I refused to play with the other children. They were ugly and broken freaks to me, and I told them as much. Only after a girl with crutches slapped me did I learn to keep quiet.

I reach the end of the plaza, follow a stone path behind the church. Bamboo steps zigzag up the hill; I take them one at a time. It gets warmer the higher I go, fewer trees and little shade. I feel slow, heavy in the light.

Up close, the shack is smaller than I remember. The concrete walls crumble at the edges, vines of brittle leaves trail down from the tin roof like networks of veins gone dry. The wood door hangs crooked, a small hole where a doorknob should be. But there is the creak of mattress springs from inside, a shuffle of footsteps. Someone takes a long, deep breath.

I knock. He says come in and I enter darkness: a black curtain hangs from the ceiling and wall to wall, splitting the room in two. There's no furniture on my side, no window, nothing. But I can hear him behind the curtain, and down below, in the space between its fraying hem and the floor, I see his brown, heavy-heeled shoes, the leather scuffed and torn at the tips.

"You're the American," he says.

I don't know if it's a question or an accusation.

"I've been waiting for you." His voice is low, a scratchy whisper.

I look at the ceiling, the walls. I don't know which way to direct my voice, so I take a step toward the curtain.

"You're good right there," he says, "right where you are." He says that he's not well, not ready to be seen, then slides a folded metal chair from his side of the room to mine. It's covered with dust, wisps of spiderweb stretching leg to leg. I leave it folded at my feet. "The nun said you're the only other American patient in the colony."

"Yes. I mean, no. Not really."

"Clarify."

I haven't had to explain myself, not for years. I was eight when my mother and I left the Philippines with the American man who would become my stepfather. Less than two years later, when the leprosy began to show, I was back. That was ten years ago.

"I lived in California," I say, "for a time."

"If that's true, then you must know the way out of here."

"That's not possible."

"There must be someone I can talk to. Some sort of boat I can take. I can bring you with me."

I close my eyes, trying to remember what I'm meant to say. "Please listen. You're very sick, and the doctors—"

"Your family must want to see you. I can get you to them."

"You need to understand. This is the best place—"

"Tell me the way out." He steps closer to the curtain,

his silhouette growing darker. "Please," he says, "tell me," and when I say no he reaches for something and throws it against the floor, shards of glass spilling toward my feet. "Get me off this goddamn island!"

I don't bother with goodbye.

I hurry down the hill, skipping steps and almost falling, then run up another, until I am as high as I can go. From here, I can see the fenced perimeter of the colony, the guards at the front gate. I can see the rectangle of the plaza, the hospital and the church, the window of my dormitory room. Beyond is the rest of the island, beyond that the empty stretch of sea.

MOST EVENINGS, I AM THE first at dinner and the first to leave. It's nearly impossible to sit alone, and the surrounding conversations are full of the same complaints, patients comparing their pains, as if there is valor in hurting more than anyone else. But if you're physically able to eat in the cafeteria, it means you can walk and sit up, lift a spoon to your lips. In Culion, a doctor once told me, there's little else a body needs to do.

Tonight, there's a shortage of rice and the food lines grow longer, the patients hungry and irritable. The air is warm and damp from all that's boiling in the kitchen, and members of the church choir practice in the corner, their hymns loud and off-tune. But Sister Marguerite insists I keep her company, and wants to go over my meeting with the American, asking new questions no matter how many times I tell it. "Did he mention Olongapo City?" she asks. "He'd spent time there, I believe, just like you."

"He didn't mention it."

"Then perhaps you can talk to him about it, the next time you see him. Share your own experiences there."

"I don't remember very much," I say.

"If you think about it tonight, then tomorrow you could—"

"I was too young when I left."

"Nothing is lost to us forever. Not if you try." As she speaks, she plucks bone from a piece of boiled fish, lining them one by one on the rim of her plate. My first week of eating in the cafeteria, a fish bone lodged itself in an old man's throat. No one heard his gulps of air, his struggle to let them out. By the time I tugged at a nurse's arm and told her what was happening, his head lay still beside his plate, eyes wide open and lips barely parted, as though he had just witnessed something too remarkable for words.

"I'm tired," I say. "Good night." But before I can leave, a group of patients stops at our table, saying that they heard about my meeting with the American. More patients gather, even a few nurses, and now the questions begin—*When will he join us? Can he get us things from the States? Tell us the color of his eyes.* A decade ago, my arrival caused the same excitement, news that an American girl had been sent to the colony. But what they found was a darkly complected Filipina, nothing special, just a girl like any other here.

"He thinks there is a boat," I say, "one that will take him away from here." I tell them it's the same boat we all imagined when we first arrived, the one we dreamed could carry us away from Culion until we realized it would have nowhere to go, because no port or shore in the world would welcome us. Someone hard of hearing asks me to repeat my answer, but I just make my way out. I've said more than enough.

SISTER MARGUERITE USED TO SAY that each person has his own unique journey to Culion.

Some are sent by families who will no longer have them, others collected from leprosariums and clinics. Many are rounded up like criminals by police, taken from their hiding places, and shipped off to the colony like cargo.

But I don't know what my journey was, the ways I came to get here. All I remember is being sick in California, and waking from a fever days later in the colony, in a room full of dying girls. My mother stayed by my side that entire day, and she told me how beautiful it was on Culion. *Palm trees along the water,* she whispered, staring out the window. *Just like California. Just like home.* She took my hands and squeezed them tight, and I felt cold against the touch of her rubber gloves. The next day, she was gone. I will not see her again.

This is what I wake from tonight, but I stopped wishing for her, stopped missing her, a long time ago.

For two days I stay in my room. I eat bread and shreds

of dried papaya, drink water from the sink. The bag of oranges is still on my floor—I'd forgotten to bring it to the American—and against the pale gray tile, the fruit looks bright and sweet. Once, in the middle of the night, I wake up famished, and I come close to eating one. But in the morning, I line them along my windowsill and sketch them instead.

This afternoon, I find a plastic container of food at my door. Attached is a note, unsigned but written in Sister Marguerite's hand, explaining that the American will not eat, that he will accept food only if I bring it to him, and that it's vital for him to keep up his strength. *I remember that you were the same way*, the note says. *I think that's very interesting, don't you?*

It's true that she was the only one I would talk to after my mother left, that she spoon-fed me when I was too weak to feed myself. Sometimes I don't know if I should thank or resent her for that; if she hadn't bothered, then I might have died, and then I wouldn't be here.

THIS TIME I DON'T KNOCK, but when I enter he's already on his side of the room. I walk to the curtain and set the container and the oranges beneath. "You have to eat. You'll get weaker if you don't."

A pale hand reaches out, grabs the food. I hear him chew and swallow, taking quick sharp breaths in between. "Sorry," he says. "I haven't eaten in a while. I've usually got better manners than that."

"It doesn't matter. Now, if there's anything else you need—"

"Don't go." He slides the folded chair to me. There's no dust on it, no webs. "Stay for a minute. Please."

If I sit, I'll have to listen to him this time, the whole way through. If I go, then there will be no point in returning. "You can't ask me for help. Not the kind you want. Do you understand that? You can't ask me those things."

"Fine," he says.

I take the chair.

"For the record, I don't normally break things the first time I meet people."

It's only when he mentions it that I notice a shard of glass by my foot, catching the light. "You cleaned it up."

"Piece by piece. It helped pass the time. I was a radio-man in the Navy. I'm good with electronics and wires, things like that. If it was broken, they sent it to me."

"You quit the Navy."

"In a manner of speaking. After that, I made my way through Olongapo, Quezon City, Manila." Beyond the curtain I see the dark shape of his body rise from the bed, moving toward the glowing square of the window. "But I never thought I'd end up in a place like this. How long has this been here anyway?"

"Since the early 1900s. It was built by Americans."

"God bless America." I hear him strike a match. Then I hear him exhale. "And the nuns? What are French nuns doing in a leper colony in this part of the world?"

When I first arrived, I assumed they had always been here, the true natives of Culion. Only now, when he asks, do I picture them aboard an eastward boat, their habits like sails in the ocean wind. I imagine Sister Marguerite among them, glimpsing the island as the boat draws near, her destiny finally fulfilled.

"Since the beginning, they've been here."

Wisps of smoke rise, disappear against the ceiling. The curtain suddenly moves toward me; he's trying to shake my hand through it. "Just to be safe," he says. "My name's Jack."

I don't know what else to do, so I take his hand.

He tells me that he is twenty-six years old, that he was stationed on Clark Air Base when he was nineteen, and that he was often disciplined for various offenses—running card games on the naval base, taking unauthorized shore leave, stealing then selling supplies. He sounds almost proud of himself for breaking the rules. For years he drifted through the Philippines, surviving on odd jobs, money made from gambling. "Not the easiest life, but I was good at it," he says, "and I intend to make it back."

"I'll tell you this once more. There's no way off this island. Not for us."

He says nothing, and for a moment I expect him to throw something else, and I brace myself for the shattering. But he just takes a slow and deep breath, then asks for my name.

"It's Teresa," I say.

.   .   .

THE NEXT MORNING I FIND Sister Marguerite in the hospital nursery, a sleeping infant in her arms. She motions for me to enter, but I do so cautiously, and once inside I stay close to the door. "I've been thinking of you," she whispers. "Your meeting went well?"

"I brought him the food. He ate."

"You're making this easier for him. I'm sure of it."

I picture his leather shoes, the only thing I see of him, pacing back and forth along a strip of sunlight. "Maybe."

She moves from crib to crib, smiling at each baby inside, and sometimes she closes her eyes for several seconds, as if praying quickly on their behalf. But babies born in Culion have one of two possible futures: if after three years they show signs of the disease, they will be reunited with their sick mothers; if no signs appear, if they are perfectly healthy, then they will be sent to a Manila orphanage, unnamed and undocumented so they can never know who or what they've come from.

I don't know which future she is praying for.

"Sister"—I take a step forward, whispering so I won't disturb the babies—"when you first sailed to Culion, do you remember seeing the island?"

She nods.

"And what did you think?"

She glances at the floor for a moment, as though she'll find her answer there. "It was night when we arrived. The island looked like a shadow. But I knew it was my place, that I was meant to be here."

"And you have no regrets? You never wanted to leave?"

"You don't question a calling. You obey it."

One of the babies cries from his crib. Sister Marguerite moves toward me, asks me to take the one in her arms. I've been in remission for three years. The doctors say I am of no harm to anyone. But I stand still, arms at my side.

"Hold her," she says. "Please."

I take the baby. She sleeps soundly but I can barely feel her, as though I'm carrying air.

"Did he say anything else?" Sister Marguerite asks. "Will he join us soon? He can't stay in that shack forever."

I rock the baby, just barely. She shifts, yawns without sound. "He still wants to leave."

Sister Marguerite sighs. "So do they all."

She's wrong. Few patients ever think of leaving. Their wish for escape, their longing for a world beyond the colony gates, died long ago. But here in the nursery, the truth is undeniable. I hear it when they cry for their mothers, for where they ought to be. And now I feel the weight of it moving, waking in my arms.

IN THE AFTERNOON, A GROUP of children waits outside my dormitory. I know them from when Sister Marguerite convinced me to give them drawing lessons, a way for me to contribute to the colony. "We drew these for the American," one of them says. "Will you give them to him?" There are pictures of rocket ships, men with wings, children as tall as trees. One shows a family, arms linked and afloat above rooftops.

I roll them up like a scroll. "I'll bring them," I say.

I knock twice when I arrive, tell him it's me. When I enter, I find the chair unfolded and upright. At some point, he was here on my side, the curtain drawn, and light let in.

I slip the drawings to his side of the room. "Some of the children drew these for you."

I hear him unroll the pictures, going through them one by one. "They're great. Tell them I said thanks."

Moments pass in silence, neither of us moving in our places. A slant of light stretches from the half-closed door, grazing the edge of my arm. Beside me, the black curtain is like a wall, so dark and solid I feel I could lean against it.

He moves closer to the curtain. "So you lived in California. I'm from a town called Tulare. Do you know it?"

"I don't. Sorry."

"For a while I lived in Santa Monica."

"Santa Monica?"

"Yeah. You've been?"

I may have, once. If I'm right, it was near the ocean, with a pier on one end of the beach. "I've heard of it," I tell him, and I can see myself sitting on the shore with my legs stretched out, my hands wrist-deep in the sand. I'm eight or nine years old, and I can feel the ocean current pulling me in. But I'm not afraid, because the tide always carries me back, as if it knows where I belong. "There's a pier in Santa Monica?"

"Yeah. With lots of rides and games, like a county fair."

I can picture those, too. "Then yes. I was there."

A breeze comes through the door, an unexpected chill. I get up to shut it, and when I look back, his hand appears just beneath the curtain, holding an orange. One half in shadow, one half in light. Like a distant sun, in the midst of eclipse.

"I saved one of them. We can split it."

"Those were meant for you."

"It's a piece of fruit. No big deal. Besides, my nails aren't so strong. Maybe you could peel it for me."

I return to my chair, pick the fruit up from the floor. I dig my thumbnail into the rind, peel it back, the scent of orange rising like mist. In California, my mother would peel them for me, removing the rind in a single spiral. I'd wind it around my wrist like a bracelet, which would always make her laugh.

I pass the fruit beneath the curtain. "Take half," he says, and without argument, I separate the fruit with my thumbs and pass him his share. Then I peel off a segment, take a small bite. It's sour and sweet and acidic, a taste so strong it overwhelms me; my eyes begin to water and I wipe them dry.

"Thank you, Jack," I say.

We say very little as we eat, but the sound of his voice—his clear and perfect American English—returns me to that moment on the shore. In my years on Culion, I've thought of it before, but I never knew if it was a memory or a dream, something conjured up in the fever from my first days in the colony. But now I know it was true, and I'm remembering other things too: the city traffic that once lulled me to sleep, the shouts of kids on a playground, the taste and feel of ice. And when the American says nothing, it's almost enough just to hear him breathe on the other side of the curtain.

The following morning, I bring him a bowl of guavas, then slices of mango in the afternoon. I do the same thing the next day, and my afternoon visit goes well into the dinner hour. It's dark by the time I start down the hill, but I find my way back; that's how well I know the path between us.

HE TELLS ME THERE ARE things he needs. A razor. Cigarettes. A newspaper in English, if I can find one. I tell him about our general store, and he sets down several bills on the floor beneath the curtain—some American, some Philippine, all of it worthless. He doesn't know that the colony has its own currency, a way of preventing anything we might touch from escaping into the world. The first time I saw a Culion coin, I kept staring at the words *Bureau of Health* spelled out along the edge. It looked like play money from a board game.

I take the money, and tell him I'll do what I can.

In the plaza, several men are building what looks like a small stage, and a few young girls are kneeling on the ground, making a large banner and smaller signs. Sister Marguerite is supervising, and as I approach her, I see the children's message: *Welcome*. Peace Corps volunteers are visiting in a week, she explains, and the colony wants to celebrate their arrival. They come once every few years, bearing gifts of medicine, bandages, crates of canned meat that barely last us a week, and they are always eager to fix broken things—faulty pipes in the kitchen, power lines knocked down by storms. And every time we honor them like heroes, but, even in their protective clothing, they keep their distance from us.

"Will we tell them about the American?" I ask.

"For what? So they can return him to the States, send him back to the Navy? He needs to be cared for, not punished." She says the doctors, even the colony administrators, agree on this. "For better or worse, he's one of us." I nod and turn to leave, but she takes my wrist and asks about the cash in my hand, plucks a bill from between my fingers and holds it up to the light, staring at it like it's a postcard from a faraway and wondrous place. "Real money," she says. "There's so much the American still doesn't know." She gives back the bill. "But he has you, Teresa. You're the best person to teach him about this life." Behind her, one girl finishes a sign and begins another. Her fingers are merely nubs now, the marker trembling as she spells out *Thank You.*

"I hope the volunteers have a lovely visit," I tell her. As if I won't be here.

HE KNOWS MY FOOTSTEPS; BEFORE I knock or speak he calls my name and tells me to come in. The curtain is swaying when I enter, as if he was on my side of the room only moments ago, then crossed over to his when he heard me approach.

I sit in my chair, set a paper bag on the floor and he reaches out, takes it. He asks how I was able to get everything he needed, so I tell him about the merchant boats that occasionally come to the colony, supplying our store with American products. "But the boats won't have you," I tell him, before he can become hopeful. "You would never be allowed on board."

"I wasn't thinking it," he says. But when I see his silhouette rise from the bed and move toward the window, he looks like a man attempting escape. And if I turned away for just a moment he could be gone, leaving me alone with the black curtain and the empty space behind it.

"You always leave," I say. "The Navy. California. All those cities in the Philippines."

He paces the length of the curtain, as if trying to figure out a response. "I guess it's a habit. One I'll have to break in Culion. But you've made it your home."

He has no right to say that, and for a moment I'm tempted to lift the curtain, flood the room with light, and tell him so. But where else would home be? California? Olongapo City? Wherever in the world my mother is? Even if I could somehow find my way back, those places would be closed off to me, and then where would I go?

"I've done what I've had to do," I say.

"What's your story?" he asks. "You know mine now."

I say nothing.

"It's okay," he says. "You can tell me." He moves closer to the curtain, his voice drawing me into the blackness, and yet I think I might be safe, that there is no danger in the deep.

I give him what he wants.

I begin with what I remember first: how my mother and I survived in the Olongapo slums, doing whatever we could for money, even when it meant hiding lepers in our tenement apartment for whatever they could pay her. *Don't touch them,* she said, *don't even look at them, and you'll be all right.* Later, when she met my stepfather, an American soldier stationed in the Philippines, she saw him as a rescue from our life, a guarantee for citizenship, and we left with him for California. My mother promised we would never go back, but one afternoon, less than two years later, she noticed wrinkled patches of skin on my forearms, purple sores on my legs. It was then, I'm sure of it, that my mother began planning the journey to Culion, knowing she would let me go, that she would never return.

"What was the last thing she said to you?" he asks.

I answer but he doesn't hear me. So I say it again. "She said she hoped that I would die quickly."

He doesn't speak, and I feel I should be ashamed by what I've just told him, for cheating him out of what could have been an exchange of happy-ending stories from home. But I don't apologize. Instead we sit, Jack and me, the only Americans in the colony. And when he hears me weep, he offers me a handkerchief beneath the curtain, his initials embroidered in the corner.

"You're the only one who'd offer me this," I say.

"You're the only one who'd take it." And when I do, his fingers curl up around my hand, and he raises it, lifting the curtain just a bit. Light from his side pours into mine. He fits his fingers in between my own, explores the curve of my wrist, the deep lines of my palm. I press my thumb into his hand, feel his skin move over bone. Then the darkness takes his form as he leans into the curtain and into me, his forehead resting against mine, and I think that maybe this is the warmth of flesh; long since forgotten, perhaps something I never, ever knew.

TODAY, IN PREPARATION FOR THE Peace Corps visit, the colony cleans. Patients and staff alike move through the plaza with dustpans and brooms. Children polish the knobs and hinges of every door. But I don't help. Instead, I stay in my room and draw, beginning with a faint line for what will be the shore, a trace of waves for what will become the sea. I feel the sand of that beach again, I feel the way Jack's hand held mine, and I draw for hours.

Later, I show him. "Is that the place? Did I get it right?"

"The Santa Monica Pier. That's how I remember it."

"I worried the pier was on the wrong side of the beach."

"It's perfect. Really." He flips through my sketchbook, looking at my drawings, impressed with every one. Then he sets it down on the floor, and turns to a blank page. "Draw yourself," he says.

I have never done a self-portrait. Except by doctors, I haven't been photographed since arriving in the colony. There is no mirror in my room, and I turn away from any window I pass to avoid my reflection.

"Come on," he says, "I want to see you."

I look down at the page, at all that empty space, imagining the movement of the pencil, the ways it will travel along the paper to arrive at a face. "If I do it," I say, "will you describe yourself, and let me draw your picture too?"

I stare into the curtain, waiting for an answer. Finally, he says, "Deal."

I pick up the sketchbook. I start with a faint oval, add a few sharp lines to show the texture of bone, then soften them to make them flesh. Below the eyes the cheeks are round, the mouth full and wide. The black hair parts in the middle, falling past the shoulders, framing the face. "Your turn," I say.

He describes his eyes, the right a bit sleepier than the left. His hair is brown, short but wavy, curling just above his ears. He has a square jaw and thin lips, a tiny scar that crosses the cleft in his chin. I go back and forth between us, shading in lines and erasing mistakes, his voice guiding my hand the entire time.

It's past dark now; I finish by candlelight. I set the picture down on the floor, my face on his side, his on mine. Two people stare back at us, together, alive on the page. "When I hear your voice," he says, "that's the girl I see."

. . .

IT'S RAINING WHEN I WAKE, all morning long, then all afternoon, so hard that everyone stays indoors. I don't go out either, and I don't see Jack; the path uphill would be too muddy, the steps too slick to climb. But with the plaza deserted, it's not so difficult to imagine him walking through it, or sitting on the edge of the fountain, watching children play their games with shells and stones.

I take my sketchbook and try to draw that scene.

But there is no rain the next morning, and I'm eager to be out, so for once I am early for my checkup at the hospital. I sign in at the front desk, and the nurse stares at me, like I'm different from the times she has seen me before. "You're the friend of the American?" she asks. I nod, and she tells me that he has just checked in as well, and is waiting to be seen by a doctor. "Fourth door on the left"—she points—"if you'd like to say hello."

I look toward the hallway, at the ceiling and floor, the walls and doors—all of it white. Somewhere down there, he sits. I could stand here, wait for him to pass me by, say nothing; he would never know it was me. Or I could go to him and open the door, and finally say hello.

I walk slowly, counting off doorknobs until I reach the fourth. I grab hold of it but I'm not ready to enter, so I stand on my toes and peer through the small window of the door. His back is to me, but I can see his hair really is a shade of brown.

I open the door. He turns to look at me, and now I

know we lied. His left eye is swollen shut. His face, neck, and shoulders are covered with lesions, his arms purple and black with open sores. And his left hand, the one he must have hidden from me, is nearly gone, the fingers curled into themselves, the remaining nails yellow and chipped.

No smile or hello. I let him think that I am just another patient, one who has wandered in by mistake. I mean to apologize, to excuse myself and leave, but all I can do is breathe. We look at each other, at our sameness, for just a moment more.

I long for the black curtain, for the fabric to rise like a tide and drown us both in darkness.

I close the door, hurry down the hall to the front desk. The nurse takes me to a room filled with a dozen other patients, and when it's my turn, two doctors examine the patches of warped and hardened flesh covering my arms and legs, the lesion scars on my chest and neck. They touch the places on my face where skin and muscle used to be. Then they look at me and tell me that I'm fine.

A DAY PASSES WITHOUT SEEING him, then two. When I finally visit, he asks why I've been gone so long. I tell him that it's a busy time in the colony, that I'm helping to pre-pare for the volunteers' arrival. Then I excuse myself, wish him a good night.

He didn't mention what happened at the hospital. He never knew who that girl was.

. . .

BEFORE THE PEACE CORPS VOLUNTEERS pass through
the colony gate, they put on gloves and surgical masks.
When they enter, doctors and nurses shake their hands, and
a group of nuns led by Sister Marguerite bow their heads
in thanks as they walk by. The smallest children run toward
them with welcome banners and signs, but this time the volunteers don't back away. They bend down, pat their heads,
offer toothbrushes and small bars of soap as presents.

I don't know if the American can see us down here, what
his view from his side of the shack might be like. But one day
soon he will draw the curtain and step out of that room, take
the path downhill. It won't be long before we're face-to-face,
and when he hears my voice, he will know exactly who I am.

One more person approaches the gate, the military
escort for the volunteers, a big, dark-haired man with eyebrows so thick his eyes are like shadows. He puts on a mask
and gloves too, but with the holster at his side he looks more
like a criminal, and no one approaches him.

Except me. I welcome him, thank him for coming, and
he blinks in surprise; I don't know if it's my good English
or my face that startles him. But before he can speak I tell
him about the American, a lost soldier far from home. I
explain how sick he is, and that he must return to California because we have done all we can for him. He looks at
me skeptically, but I keep talking, and even I can hear the
plea in my voice. "Look around. There's nothing for him

here." Then I take his gloved hand and lead him several steps toward the church, and point to the top of the hill behind it, where the American hides.

TWO DAYS LATER, A PAIR of Peace Corps volunteers walks with Jack through the colony, crowds of patients looking on. A white towel is draped over his head, obscuring his face. I never told the military escort that he was AWOL, and yet the escort walks close behind, hand on his holster, as though he's watching over a prisoner who might escape. When they near the end of the plaza, Jack shifts his head from side to side, like he is searching for me, and for a moment I think of calling out to him. Maybe this is how we start again, in daylight, no curtain between us.

But then he moves on. Across the plaza Sister Marguerite watches, and when he passes her by she turns in my direction, a mix of pity and worry on her face, like something terrible has happened to me, or very soon will. She starts to come my way but I leave, walking toward the church, then up the hill to the shack.

The curtain is gone now, just a black pile of cloth in the corner on the floor, and now I see what I couldn't before—a thin mattress on a sagging cot, a bucket half-filled with water, a tin cup beside it, the children's drawings rolled up like scrolls. Pieces of rind are scattered on the floor, but they still smell of the orange we ate. I pick them up, line them along the windowsill.

Sitting on the edge of the cot, I stare out the window and draw the sails of merchant ships in the distant water, the thin cords of clouds above them. I draw the sky, the faint daylight moon, whatever is in front of me. I finish the picture before dark.

Superassassin

September 1958. Coast City, California. The noble alien Abin Sur, protector of sector 2814 of our galaxy, crash-lands on Earth. Buried beneath the rubble of his spacecraft, he uses his last flicker of energy to summon test pilot Hal Jordan and offers him the fabled Ring of Power, a weapon created by the Guardians of Oa. With his dying breath Abin Sur asks, "Will you be my successor, Hal Jordan? Will you swear to use this ring to uphold justice throughout the universe?"

"I swear it," Jordan promises. He slips the ring onto his finger, and takes the Guardians' Oath:

> Let those who worship evil's might
> Beware my power—Green Lantern's Light!

For nearly four decades Hal Jordan will save the universe on countless occasions as the Green Lantern, one of Earth's greatest champions. But in the 1990s, just years from the new millennium, he turns on the Guardians, and becomes the most powerful villain in the galaxy. The question remains: Did the Green Lantern die a villain or a hero? This question has stumped historians in recent years. This essay will retrace the history of the Green Lantern, and conclude once and for

Black ink streaks across my paper when Brandon De-Stefano swipes it from my desk. "May I?" he asks. His eyes rush side to side over my words. "Listen to this crazy shit," he tells Tenzil Jones, his best friend. Brandon reads my paper to Tenzil in what is supposed to be my voice, adding an accent that isn't mine. Then he looks up at me, shaking his head in disapproval. "It's supposed to be about a real person in history, freak. What's wrong with you?"

"Hey," Tenzil whispers from behind me, "maybe I'll do mine on the Tooth Fairy."

I don't waste my time with talk. I put my hand out for the paper's return. Brandon makes sure that Mr. Cosgrove isn't looking and then crumples my paper, hurling it at me like a grenade. It hits my face and falls dead to the ground. "Kapow!" Brandon says, pointing his finger at me like a gun. "Why didn't you use your power ring to stop it?" Tenzil holds up his palm, and the two high-five each other, as if they've accomplished some great feat of teamwork.

"You are no Dynamic Duo," I tell them.

"What?" Brandon asks.

"You are"—I lean into him, aligning my eyes with his—

"no Dynamic Duo." I say each word slowly, every syllable getting equal time. It's not my place to make terrible truths easier to hear; all I do is reveal them.

Suddenly Tenzil's finger flicks my ear, fast and hard. My neck jerks, my back stiffens. I feel the heat just below my right temple. "You're whacked, man," he says.

I know better than to tell Mr. Cosgrove. Not because I'm afraid; I just prefer another kind of justice.

I pick up my essay from the floor, pulling at opposite corners to undo the crumpled mass. It's wrinkled, like old skin, so I rub it between my hands, up and down until my palms burn from friction. When the page is smooth, I continue to write, even after the bell rings and the classroom has emptied. Only when Mr. Cosgrove starts locking up windows and shutting mini-blinds do I stop.

"Mr. Cosgrove?" He can't hear me above his whistling, so I say his name again.

"What? Oh, sorry." He turns to me. "Didn't realize you were here."

"I know." I start erasing the chalkboard for him. "I just wanted to tell you that I'm excited about this assignment. I think I'll learn a lot from this."

He nods. "I'm sure you will."

"I used to hate your class, this subject."

"History changes," he says.

"And I used to hate you."

For four seconds Mr. Cosgrove is silent. Then he says, "I guess we all change then, don't we?" He looks me in the eye, smiling, and after some moments of examination, I decide the smile is real, so I nod in return.

I wipe chalk dust from my shirt and offer to help him with the windows, but he says they've been done, and explains that he needs to get home soon. I grab my backpack from my chair, and before I leave, I tell him that his class is my favorite, the only one that's useful in the real world.

LONG BEFORE THE HECKLING FROM classmates, the questioning stares from old churchwomen, and long, long before I knew the true story of my father, I was aware of the strange mutant abilities that my body possesses: though my skin is fair, I never burn in the sun, can barely manage a midsummer tan. When seasons change, so does the color of my hair, back and forth from brown to black. Despite my roundish face I have a unique bone structure that captures both shadow and light in just the right places, so that in the proper lighting my face can be startling. And my eyes—somewhere between slanted gashes and perfect ovals—are of two colors: the right is as brown as wet earth, and the left is jet black, a perfect obsidian orb. I keep them behind slightly tinted eyeglasses.

Fifteen years ago, at the moment of my spawning, no one could have guessed the potency of my hybridity.

"What are you goofing about now?" Luc asks me. He is quick to interrupt my meditations, dismissing them as daydreams. He shoots a rubber band at me from across the table. It bounces off my right lens. When I tell him to quit, to stop or I will kill him, I am shushed by the librarian, who frowns at me like an archenemy whose plans I have just foiled. "You're zoning out again," Luc says, sliding his grammar book over to me. "You said you would help me, so help." Though Luc is the most intelligent and perceptive student in the ninth grade (and the only other person I've ever known who is able to comprehend the theories of an antimatter universe), his counselor insists that he take ESL classes. His English, standardized testing says, is not up to speed. In grade school they said the same thing about me. I knew the words—I had a tenth-grade vocabulary by the time I was eight. I simply chose not to speak.

We muddle through the textbook examples of the passive voice, and I even devise my own exercises, in comic-book format. *"Superman has been killed mercilessly by me," proclaimed Doomsday.* But today I am in no mood to be a champion of standard written English. "Later," I promise. Luc shrugs, thinking that I have given up, that surrendering is a possibility. So I rescue the moment by suggesting "Dystopia?" and his frown morphs into a smile. In a flash we cram books into our backpacks, slip on our raincoats, and pull hoods over our heads. As we exit the library, the words "psychos," "faggots," and "losers" reach us from behind study carrels. Luc and I stop to face our accusers, giving them looks we will substantiate when the time is right. Then we are out the library door, off the campus, and under the afternoon drizzle. We stand at the bus stop, two secret heroes on the fringes of winter, waiting for the sun, any source of rejuvenation, just one outbound bus away from here and into the city.

DYSTOPIA COMICS IS THE ONLY all-used-comic-book store in town. Most stores file away their back issues in neat alphabetized rows, each one sealed in a plastic bag. But Dystopia lives up to its name. Comics are stuffed into shoddy cardboard boxes, and Luc and I spend hours rummaging through bin after bin. In the past half hour Luc has found issues of *Justice League* and *Sandman,* even a water-damaged issue of *The Watchmen,* and I've started a small stack of old issues of *Green Lantern,* precisely what I need for my research. I sometimes think that Luc and I possess an extra sense, an instinct for finding small treasures among the torn and the discarded.

"Closing time," a husky voice mutters from behind and above me. I do a quick one-eighty, fists clenched and ready. I face the cashier, who stands just inches away from me. His globular, fleshy belly is even closer, oozing over the elastic waistband of his Bermuda shorts. "If you're going to read it, then buy it."

I give Luc the signal and then shift my eyes back to the cashier. "Pardon me, sir," I say, "but your volume is infringing upon my space."

He blinks. "My what?"

"The amount of space your cubic units are occupying."

He blinks again. "So?" I've confused him, thrown him

off, and all he can do is point to the clock. "Just hurry it up, all right?"

My eye catches the exposed belly once more. With the proper serrated edge I could carve a tunnel right through it.

I smile at the mass before me. "Let's go, Luc."

We walk out the door and turn the corner into a narrow alley. We crouch down to the ground, shielded between Dumpsters, and Luc unzips his backpack. From between textbooks and folders he pulls out our stack of comics. "Distract him longer next time," he says. "He almost turned around too soon."

"No back talk from the sidekick." I go through the comics and take what's mine.

The rain has stopped. Still, we don our hoods. We proceed into the street outside the crosswalk lines, defying the blinking red hand before us. "Nice work," I tell Luc. "See you tomorrow, oh seven hundred hours."

"Oh seven hundred hours," he confirms.

ON SAD NIGHTS MY MOTHER listens to her 45 rpm of "Johnny Angel" over and over again until she passes out. Tonight is going to be one of those nights. Before I can even lock the door behind me, she starts screaming, asking where I've been. "Nowhere," I tell her. "Just out."

"And what should I do if something happened to you out there?" she asks, one hand on her hip, the other tugging at the neckline of her Las Vegas sweatshirt. "What should

I do then?" She takes heavy, staggered breaths and begins to empty out the kitchen cupboards, throwing food we need over the fire escape, weeping, uttering profanities about men and why they are the way they are.

I give her five quick shots of Johnnie Walker and put her to bed. I take off her shoes, pull the sheets over her, and press REPLAY on her turntable. She puts her arms around my neck and pulls my face to hers, telling me what a good boy I've been. "Don't you change," she whispers. I can feel the tears on her lips wetting my ear.

"Go to sleep, Mom," I whisper. I pull down the shades, shutting out the last bits of daylight.

She got left again. I knew my mother was feeling hopeful this time around. This guy lasted almost four weeks.

When I warn her, she tells me I'm crazy, so this time I kept quiet. But I saw it coming. Her strategy was faulty: she had been making domestic offerings—a home-cooked meal of lumpia and pinakbet, Filipino delicacies she calls her love potions. But they lack any magical properties. Her men always see the food as alien and weird, a little too far from home. So they take what they want and vanish. "Ride a rocket to the moon, that's fine," she once slurred to some guy on the phone, "but baby, won't you please come back?" It was my twelfth birthday party, but I wasn't the one who wanted him there. I took the receiver from her hands. "Accidents happen, bastard," I warned, "so watch your back." She grabbed the phone, hit me with it, and then apologized for my rudeness. But he'd already hung up.

Mom's messed-up universe started with one bad star: a nine-month marriage to the man who was my father. He brought her to the States, a living knickknack from his military days. Their union, brief as it was, spawned me and all my biological peculiarities. "You're like Aquaman," Luc said when I told him the story—"cool." But Aquaman's mother was a mermaid, his father a human being. Nothing is human within the man who was my father. He disappeared from her life just hours before I was born. What I imagine, what I've even dreamed, is that he is a sinister breed of assassin, with white hair, white skin, and white eyes, invading alien streets, sent to find and fuck my mother and then finish her off. When she's drunk, she talks about my origin, sticking the sick story in my head, panel after panel after panel.

And then she'll break in half, Johnny Angel and Johnnie Walker to the rescue. But I forgive her. Like all heroes, she needs her Fortress of Solitude, her Paradise Island, any place tucked away from the evil in the world. Not to worry: I keep a lookout.

IN THE MORNING, I KNOCK on my mother's door, three times, but she's out cold. She's already late for work, so I go into her bedroom and lay her pink waitress's uniform on a chair. I whisper goodbye and then leave for school.

Luc meets me on the corner. "Ready?" I ask.

He opens his backpack. "It's all here."

"Good," I nod. "Let's go."

We have our enemies. Today Luc and I will deliver Brandon DeStefano to justice.

Last week we were reading comics at lunch on the football-field bleachers when Brandon and Tenzil walked by. "It's Luc the Gook!" Brandon screamed. I gave him the finger, and Luc told him to run along with the other non-sentients. "Non*what*?" Brandon said, climbing up toward us, bleacher by bleacher. "I don't understand Korean, gook." Then Tenzil reached from behind and snatched Luc's comic, an almost valuable issue of *Swamp Thing* #12. He tossed it to Brandon, who stuffed it down the back of his pants, farted on it, and then dropped it in a puddle beneath the bleachers. "Freaks," he said. Then they walked toward the lunch court-yard, a trail of sinister *ha-ha-ha*'s ricocheting behind them.

Luc went down to rescue the comic, but I was still watching when his head started twitching, shoulder and ear crashing against each other. His spine arched him for-ward and back, forward and back, each vertebra breaking through skin until the body was no more. Then, in a sudden flash of light, Brandon DeStefano became The Gas, a force able to release methane-based emissions powerful enough to stun an enemy or wipe out an entire planet. Luc and I vowed revenge. I intend to get it.

We get to school early, while the boys' locker room is still empty. We find The Gas's locker, and in seventy-four seconds Luc picks the lock. I pull the impostor Right Guard deodorant from my backpack and make the switch.

Later, when PE is over, Luc and I dress quickly, taking

positions by our lockers. We keep an eye out for The Gas, who has just emerged from the showers. He comes closer and closer but pays us no mind. In regular street clothes we are anonymous, merely mortal men.

The Gas dries himself off and reaches into his locker for his deodorant. He shakes the can once, twice, and removes the cap. He raises his arm above his head, positioning the Right Guard at his armpit. Before he can spray, Luc and I vanish.

The Gas has no idea of the power that's about to befall him; no one ever does. First my enemies underestimate me; then I smash them.

"DO YOU THINK IT'LL HEAL?" On this team Luc is the conscience.

"No one has ever died from a scorched armpit," I tell him, stashing another swiped teacher's edition in my locker. He knows I speak the truth. I don't say things just to be reassuring.

The final bell rings. By tomorrow morning we'll hear snippets of talk here and there about the incident. Campus security will circulate in homerooms and PE classes, spouting the same refrain: if we work together, we can prevent this from happening again.

Feeble heroism from the crooked authorities. This is what they said last time and the time before that, and no one suspected our true identities then. "We ought to celebrate," I decide. "Meet me at Kingpin Donuts before school tomorrow."

Luc stares into my eyes as if he means to challenge me. "You said you would change the deodorant into spray paint, not a blowtorch," he whispers. "You said you wouldn't do this anymore."

"Silence." I slam my locker shut. "We're done for today. Go home."

AFTER SCHOOL I CHECK ON my mother at the restaurant. I take my station on an adjacent rooftop, over what was once a tropical fish store. Four months ago the store was bombed—newspapers suspected a Filipino gang—and the next day I walked by to find half the storefront missing. I entered and walked among the ruins, the crunch of aquarium shards beneath my feet. Ruby- and sapphire- and emerald-colored fish lay lifeless on the ground, but still reflected the brilliant sun in each tiny scale. I stuffed as many as I could into the front pocket of my backpack and took them home, tucked them in the freezer behind the ice trays and TV dinners. Late at night I'd take them out and hold each one to the light; they were like life-giving stones, alien and cold. When Mom found them, their color had finally faded, and she flushed them down the toilet.

From up here I can see down into the restaurant, beyond the yellow-lettered window, which reads CLARK'S PLACE though the owners are a Vietnamese couple by the name of Ngoc-Tran. "They probably needed something catchier, for business purposes," Luc said, explaining why they used the name. "Koreans do it all the time."

So do superheroes.

The last of the afternoon regulars finally leaves, and my mother takes a cigarette break at a corner booth. She stares out at the street, taking greedy drags of a Marlboro. She exhales smoke against the window, and it dances before her face like some sort of phantom lover. I often catch my mother in these moments, a sad woman in pink, looking into nothing, waiting. "That's how I met your father," she once confessed in a stupor. She was one of Manila Rosie's Beauties, the best dancing girls the Navy boys could find in the city. "And I was your daddy's favorite," she said. After a two-week courtship he proposed to my mother, promising her citizenship in the USA. "United Stars of America" is what she called it. I have had longing dreams about this incarnation of my mother, seeing her asleep and afloat in outer space, the constellations re-forming themselves around her. I try to locate this part of her in myself, to isolate it from all the other stuff.

Then suddenly, from nowhere, a man in a uniform invades the picture. He sits down at her booth, lights my mother another cigarette, lights his own. They begin to talk. I don't need to hear what they're saying; I can read the words, frame by frame. My mother laughs, her hand over her breast, as if she is gasping for air. She is weakening.

Oh, stop! You're too much, do you know that? she says.

He tosses his head back, his shoulders bouncing up and down, up and down, laughing at his own jokes with a villain's arrogance. Then he grabs my mother's hand and brings it close to his face. He is acquainting himself with my mother's biology, remembering the texture of her skin, her scent. *My little tropical gardenia,* he says to her. But I can read the thought bubbles above his head. *So easy. This bitch will be so easy.*

I'm too far and high up above. There's no way to warn her in time, no hope for a last-minute rescue.

In 1976 the Green Lantern returns to the stars. This is a difficult time for him. Realizing that he is unable to wipe out evil on Earth and the societal ills of the era, he falters in his ability to wield the power ring. He is summoned to Oa, where the Guardians put him on trial and consider finding a replacement. The following dialogue is an excerpt from that trial:

"Perhaps Abin Sur was mistaken in selecting you, Hal Jordan."

"Please, Guardians. Allow me to prove myself worthy of the ring. Allow me to be your champion once more."

The world jerks to a stop, and my pencil slips from my hands. I pick it up from the littered bus floor. "Brake more gently next time!" I shout to the bus driver. Baldie shoots me a look from his extended rearview mirror.

He does it again at the next stop. "Hey!" I rise from my seat. "I said brake more gently next time!" I walk toward the front. "Did you hear me?" Baldie ignores me and slams on the brakes at the light. I keep him in my eye as I fight gravity, but I lose my footing; I fall. But just as quickly I'm up again, and I almost manage to dig the point of my pencil into his arm, but two of his henchmen passengers force me off before I can make contact with his skin. I walk the rest of the way home against traffic so loud that it smothers the battle cries in my head.

WHEN I CALL, LUC'S GRANDMOTHER picks up the phone. I don't bother identifying myself; she always drops the receiver at the sound of my voice, and I have to wait two or three minutes until Luc finds out it's for him. To his grandmother, I'm The Filipino, the mutant friend who is too different for her to speak with, too weird to be allowed to come over.

Luc finally picks up, and I tell him what happened. "Just breathe for a sec," he says, competing with loud kitchen noises in the background. "It'll be fine."

"He had to be stopped," I explain. "He's putting other lives at risk. Better the driver die than a busload of innocents." If I have to be the one to do it, then I'll do it.

Luc understands the good of my intentions and says so. "But it's over now. You kept all those passengers safe."

"Let's hope."

Then Luc says he's sorry but he has to go, his mother needs to call his aunt about a Korean variety show on cable.

"No problemo," I say, "and thanks again. Old chum."

WITH MY MOTHER AT THE restaurant, I have time to work in my lab. I can construct bombs and explosives, but these require the proper chemicals and materials, and I can use the bathroom for only so many hours in a day before my mother becomes suspicious. When she pounds on the door, asking what I am doing, I tell her nothing, to please give me five or ten minutes. She guesses that I am masturbating and tells me to stop. I tell her okay.

My favorite weapon is my slingshot. I stole it from a high-quality sporting goods store six months back: lightweight, aerodynamic, potential of elasticity twenty times as great as the average sling. How enraging, to think that a lesser comic like *Dennis the Menace* has reduced the slingshot to a mischief-making toy kept in a child's back pocket! People forget that David killed Goliath with a slingshot. With the proper ammunition, I could kill too.

But I am at work on what I hope will be the greatest addition to my arsenal.

Centuries ago Filipino warriors created the yo-yo as a weapon, emitting from their hands stone-heavy objects at the ends of twenty-foot-long ropes. They learned to hunt with it, to kill. Eventually the yo-yo immigrated to America. The story goes that a traveling salesman named Duncan saw one and introduced it to the country as a new hobby, a toy to pass the time.

I intend to get it back.

I will fuse together my native ingenuity with modern technology to create a weapon of the deadliest force. My yo-yo will be of marble, attached to string at least fifty feet long, so that even from rooftops I can stun my enemies far, far below. My father too had weapons. In the framed photo my mother keeps on her bureau, he holds a rifle in one hand, my mother in the other.

Suddenly I hear movement in the apartment. "Come out here!" my mother shouts, pounding on the bathroom door. "Come out and meet my new friend!"

"You're early! Hold on a sec!" I stash everything behind the toilet paper under the sink, hiding it next to the Windex and Lysol.

I open the door and find my mother standing before me, her head resting dreamily on a man's arm. "Honey," she says, smiling at me, "this is Alex. He's our mailman. We met today at the restaurant."

At least six feet tall, Lex towers over my mother and over me. He is well-postured, undoubtedly strong and agile. His uniform shows a badge of a bald eagle, and another badge tells me that he has proudly delivered U.S. mail for five years. "Hey, champ," he says. He fixes his eyes, as blue and sharp as lasers, on me. Five milky-white fingers reach out.

Armed with addresses and ZIP codes, Lex can track down anyone, anywhere. If my mother and I were to escape, he could follow the trail of our forwarding address to find us. It's the extra sense, the instinct, of a hunter.

Villain.

But I accept his challenge and take his hand. I tilt my head down just a bit, so that my glasses slide down the bridge of my nose. "Nice to meet you," I say. Lex does a double take at my nonmatching eyes. Already I have the upper hand.

MY MOTHER AND LEX WANT privacy, so tonight I'm a bedroom shut-in. But I can still hear them laughing, dancing clumsily around the front room to old Motown love songs. Luckily, I have the ability to phase out any and all distractions, to teleport my thoughts, even my senses, elsewhere. I believe this is another of my mutant abilities, the active residue of my father's genetic imprint. It's the power he used on Mom and me.

I use that power now. I have homework to do.

I'm at that difficult point in my research where Hal Jordan's status as a hero comes into question. In *Green Lantern* #50, Volume 3, he stands before a jury of Guardians, on trial for attempting to alter history in order to save his destroyed city and its murdered inhabitants. "Surrender the ring!" they say in unison. "We command you!"

And then: Hal Jordan's face. His mask. His eyes. Then nothing. Only a frightening flash of green.

I turn the page slowly, knowing what comes next: an exploding sky, fallen emerald towers, the lifeless bodies of

Guardians long thought to be immortal scattered among the debris. Hal Jordan takes their rings, all of them, and explodes into space, his eyes blank with madness and power. It's the face of a villain, the kind I've seen a million times before.

But consider what Hal Jordan has seen! Consider the burden he bears! *He got there too late.* He arrived just in time to witness his city's destruction by an enemy he couldn't defeat. You don't recover from that; you fix it. If I could rewrite the world, I'd do the same.

The following pages are panels of green: he wipes out a building in the background, **KRAZAAKK!**, one in the foreground, **BLAZAAAM!** He destroys another, and another. Then—**CRASH!**—something made of glass falls to the floor in the living room. I hear my mother and Lex whirling around to the music, bumping into bookshelves and walls, causing fragile things to fall. They laugh through loud kisses.

"Could you please be quiet out there?" They don't answer. "Would you be quiet, please?"

AT 2:43 A.M. I WAKE from weird dreams. Dehydrated and dizzy, I get a glass of milk. On the way back to my room I peek through my mother's half-closed door. She's curled up in Lex's arms. Tangled sheets bind them together.

I walk toward them, silent in bare feet, invisible in the blue glow of the digital clock. I stand at the foot of the bed, watching their bodies rise and fall with every breath. If I wanted to,

I could crawl in between them, slip my head into the circle of my mother's arms, and ram my knee into Lex's balls.

My mother mumbles something in her sleep, and slowly she turns away from Lex. I go to her. I can feel her pupils shift side to side beneath the skin of her eyelids, and I press down on them just enough until the panic in her head subsides. I move a strand of black hair away from her face, looping it slowly around my finger.

I float to the other side of the bed, over to Lex. In the moonlight he is even paler, and the stubble on his chin is like metallic bristles against my knuckles. I kneel next to him and set my head down beside his. I can see my mother's lipstick smeared along his neck, trailing down to the center of his chest. I imagine my mother kissing him, just inches above where the heart should be. I lay my palm there, just barely touching skin. I can feel the life beating inside him.

"What do you want from us?" I whisper to him. "Who sent you here?" But like my mother, he is drowned in sleep or just passed out.

So I test him. I tip my almost-empty glass, letting a tiny drop of milk fall onto his ear. The white dot slides from the outer edge and vanishes into the black hole of his ear canal. His neck and shoulders jerk, lightning-quick. Then he is still again.

"Assassin," I say. I return to the kitchen to wash my glass.

.   .   .

WE HAVE NOT SEEN THE Gas for almost two weeks since the battle. At lunch Luc and I split up, eavesdropping on conversations, trying to piece together the fate of our nemesis.

After school we regroup on the library roof. "I heard Suzy Cheerleader talking to one of the vice principals," Luc says. "Brandon's in the hospital."

"The Gas will be fine," I tell him, staring out onto the campus quad. We stay low, speaking in whispers.

"Did you hear me? He's in the hospital. His arm needs some sort of operation. Skin grafts or something. What did you put in that thing anyway?"

Skin grafts. Then the body of my enemy is mutating as well. Fascinating. "Mercury fulminate, chloride of azode, some other chemicals. The usual." I keep an eye out until I finally spot Tenzil, blanketing the school with his propaganda. I blame Tenzil, an ally of The Gas, for our corrupt student government. As vice president, he's the person who rejected my proposal for a school trip to next year's Comic Book Convention, and gave my money to varsity track instead.

I pull the yo-yo from my bag. "What the hell is that?" Luc asks.

"Quiet." This moment requires silence and the utmost precision.

Tenzil comes closer as I loop the string round and round my finger until I've cut off circulation. I raise my hand over the edge. But suddenly Luc grabs my wrist. "Don't," he says, trying to bring me back.

I take a quick foot to his stomach, freeing myself from his clutches. "If we don't get him, he'll get us."

"What are you talking about?" Luc asks, as if he doesn't already know. He reaches for my wrist again, but he's too slow: I snap my hand forward, letting go of the yo-yo for its spectacular debut.

The double disk drops straight to the ground, deadly with the force and weight of marble. But Tenzil is gone, and the yo-yo dangles at the string's end, lifeless, refusing to wind its way back up to me. "Where is he?" I say. "Where the fuck did he go?" I crane my neck over the edge, scanning the quad, the locker bay, anywhere someone might hide from me. But Tenzil is nowhere to be found. "Traitor!" I accuse Luc. But when I turn, he too is gone.

I take a quick inventory of my surroundings.

No traces.

I KEEP NO SCHOOL ID, have no driver's permit. I tossed my Social Security card once I had committed the number to memory. Anonymity keeps me safe.

I stop by Ollie's Market on the way home. Ollie stands behind the counter, a sixty-something grump in a sweat-stained undershirt, venting his frustrations to anyone who'll listen. At his side is Sasha the Amputee, Ollie's half retriever, half something else. Sasha's right hind leg was the only casualty of the last holdup, which Ollie swears, despite the ski masks, was done by Filipino gangsters.

"Filipinos!" he curses to the air. "Stealing this and stealing that!"

He makes this so easy.

My mutant biology hides that part of me he would fear. Ollie continues complaining and accusing, unaware that a shape-shifter stands before him. I tell him I know exactly how he feels, that they really can't be trusted, that they're a dangerous and deadly breed, as my hand fingers its way to the mini-rack of candy bars at my side.

But Sasha sees. The mutt snarls, her snout pointed at me, accusing me. *Go ahead,* I dare her. *Hobble after me and you'll lose another, you damaged bitch.* Mission accomplished, I tell Ollie goodbye, and press my heel onto Sasha's front paw as I walk out the door. She lets out a pathetic yelp. "Sorry." I smile at Ollie, petting the dog's head.

I exit the store and make a sharp right into an alleyway. I cross a four-way intersection diagonally, dodging cars and buses. I make a left, a right, and another right. I round corner after corner until the geometry of the city swallows me whole and it's safe for me to eat.

THE SHADES ARE DRAWN WHEN I enter our apartment. I hear movement from the bedroom. "Mom?"

I open her door. "Mom." She's on the floor, lying on her side. Laid out beside her is my father's uniform, still wrapped in plastic on a wire hanger. She reaches out to it, moving her thumb back and forth over a shiny gold button.

I give her a shot of Johnnie Walker. I pour her another and then another, and she goes on about how Lex doesn't love her, that the evil in men will always kill her, more and more slowly each time. "All the time. All the time this happens. Tell your father to stop it, please." She weeps into my chest, clinging to my shirt. Streaks of blood stain her hands. She's been cutting herself again.

An orphaned boy sees a bat flying through a window. The last son of Krypton dreams of the afterglow of his dead home world. All heroes have their omens; this blood will be mine.

"I will," I tell her. "I swear it." But she cannot hear my oath.

In conclusion, he is no longer the Green Lantern. With a final surge of power, Hal Jordan transforms himself into Parallax, a master of space and dimension. His only agenda: to destroy time, to interrupt for good the linearity of history. With one hand he will knock past, present, and future out of order; he will be the judge of who may live, who will die, and who will never have existed at all. Time will move forward, time will move back, until it collides with itself, until what is left is the Zero Hour, and all that has gone wrong can finally be set right.

Villains and heroes don't ask for the power they're given: Destiny, Fate, and Luck drop it on us like a star, and we have no choice but to use it.

Tonight I must enter the fray.

.   .   .

I PAINT BLACK AROUND MY eyes, like a domino mask, erasing the traces of who I am.

Mother's future slips into Mother's past as I don my father's uniform jacket. It fits perfectly; I never knew our bodies were the same. Gold buttons sparkle on my chest, badges adorn my arms. To the collar I attach a cape, a long piece of cloth light enough that it does not impede my speed, dark enough that it keeps me wrapped in night shadows. All superassassins rely on the darkness.

I place my ammunition—segments of aluminum pipe filled with impact-sensitive explosives—in a leather pouch attached to my belt. I secure the slingshot in my front belt loop; the yo-yo I keep in an oversized pocket on my pant leg.

Midnight strikes. I climb out the window, descend the fire escape, and run through the city, staying in back alleys and on unlit streets. I keep an eye out for any and all enemies who dare to venture into the night. Though they are many and I am one, I will fight this battle alone. I have no need for Luc anymore. Sidekicks are extraneous; they give up the fight too easily. Robin was killed off for a reason after all.

I make my way to the abandoned projects. I enter through the back, and blast open the door to the stairwell. I fly up seven, eight, nine flights. I need to go higher.

Fourteen, fifteen, sixteen flights. I must go higher.

I reach the roof. I walk along its perimeter. Night wind howls all around, blowing my cape behind me like a black ghost in tow.

I peer over the edge; the city itself has become a grid. Black streets and white sidewalks crisscross, framing city blocks like tiny pictures, a page of panels with too many scenes. But somewhere in all of this I know my enemy lurks, waiting for me to strike, daring me to cross the white borders and enter the battle. I will wait for him every night if I have to.

I take out the slingshot. I load the ammunition and pull back the sling. I aim, ready at any moment to let go.

Help

IN OUR BATTLE AGAINST THE BEATLES, IT WAS MY Uncle Willie who threw the first punch, and for that, he said, he should have been knighted. I didn't argue.

We fought them in 1966, the year they played Araneta Coliseum in Manila. They were scheduled to leave two days later, and as executive director of VIP Travel at Manila International Airport, it was Uncle Willie's job to make sure the Beatles' travel went smoothly, that no press or paparazzi detain them. But the morning after their concert, Imelda Marcos demanded one more show: a Royal Command Performance for the First Lady. When reporters asked the Beatles for their reply, they said, supposedly, "If the First Lady wants to see us, why doesn't she come up to our room for a special exhibition?" Then they walked away, all the newspapers wrote, laughing.

Uncle Willie took it hard.

He called me that night. "It's an emergency," he said, "come quick!" He hung up before I could speak, so I snuck two San Miguel beers from the refrigerator and headed out. "I'm leaving," I told my father, who was on the sofa with his feet on the coffee table, staring at an episode of *Bonanza* dubbed in Tagalog. He nodded and gave me an A-OK with his fingers. There was a bag of pork rinds on his lap and empty soda cans at his feet, and the whole room was littered with dirty plates and unwashed laundry. I even caught a glimpse of a bright pink bra that belonged to some woman he'd brought home earlier that week. We had lived like this ever since my mother left for what she called her "Vacation USA," which was going on its fourth year, despite occasional postcards promising her return. Uncle Willie was the one who watched over me, but I was sixteen now, too old to be cared for. Still, if he needed me, I was there.

I met up with my cousins, JohnJohn and Googi—they'd been summoned too—and together we headed to Uncle Willie's apartment. When we arrived, we found him at the kitchen table, fists clenched like he was ready for a fight, and he only grew angrier as he recounted the story. "Those Beatles insulted the essence of Filipina womanhood," he said. "*Special exhibition.* Scoundrels!" I told him to calm down, that the Beatles were just making a joke, but Uncle Willie said nothing was funny about Imelda Marcos. He pointed to a framed black-and-white photograph of her on top of the TV, then brought it over and made us look. "She is the face of our country. Can you see?" In the picture, Imelda Marcos was seated in a high-backed wicker chair frilled with ribbons and flowers, staring out into the distance, her queenly face shaded beneath a parasol held by an anonymous hand. The photo was a famous publicity shot—you'd see it at the mall or in schools, even some churches—but I always imagined that it was Uncle Willie holding that parasol, protecting her from a scorching sun while he did his best to endure it. He wasn't alone in his admiration for Imelda Marcos—the country still loved her back then—but Uncle Willie didn't have much else. His last girlfriend left before I was born, and the demands of his work, he said, allowed no time for another. Coordinating flights with Imelda Marcos's schedule was the closest thing he had to romance, and instead of treating his devotion with admiration and respect, our family laughed it off as a joke.

I took the picture frame from his hands and set it facedown on the table. "Yeah," I said, "I can see."

"Okay," he said, "good. Then the Beatles will pay for their insolence." He dimmed the lights and drew the curtains as though someone might be watching from afar, then sat down to reveal his plan: the next day, just before the Beatles boarded their plane, Uncle Willie would divert the Beatles' security guards and send the group to their gate, where we would be waiting, disguised as airport personnel, ready to attack. "I don't wish to maim them seriously," he said, "but we must teach them a lesson." He mapped out the scene on the table with his finger, drawing invisible X's and arrows, showing who would stand where and who would do what when it was time to strike. But where he saw battle plans I saw fingerprints streaked over a glass tabletop.

"And that," he said, "is how we will defeat the Beatles."

I looked at my cousins. They looked at me. We all looked at Uncle Willie.

"So what you're saying"—Googi leaned forward, like he was trying to make sure he heard correctly—"is that we get to meet the Beatles."

"To defeat them, yes," Uncle Willie answered.

"But again," JohnJohn said, his face suddenly serious, "we get to meet the Beatles."

Uncle Willie nodded slowly, as if they were the ones who didn't understand what was really being said.

My cousins looked at each other, then at me. "I'm in," Googi said with a clap of his hands. "I'll help you."

"Me too," JohnJohn said. "Let's beat the Beatles."

Uncle Willie turned to me. Even in the weak light, I could see the strands of his thinning gray hair, hard and slick with pomade, and the deepening folds of wrinkled skin around his eyes. He was in his late fifties then, but he looked older than he ever had before, as if I'd been away for years and was suddenly back. "You're my uncle," I said, "of course I'll help you." My cousins rolled their eyes, like I was trying to kiss up, to be a better nephew than they were.

Uncle Willie looked at each of us, took a deep and slow breath, as if this was a history-making moment to remember forever. "My men," he said, smiling proudly.

UNCLE WILLIE COOKED US A late dinner of Spam and egg fried rice, which we washed down with a case of San Miguel (he kept a supply on hand, should any of us drop by). Then he went into his bedroom and came out with a stack of pillows and sheets. We'd need a good night's rest, he said, if we were to defeat the Beatles the next day.

But only Uncle Willie went to bed; my cousins and I stayed up, gambling away what little pocket money we had in our own version of poker. "I'm going to ask Paul for an autograph," Googi said, shuffling the deck, "and I want it to say, *To Guggenheim, citizen of the world. With deepest admiration, Paul McCartney*." My cousin changed his name from Mervin to Guggenheim when he turned thirteen, believing that if you were named after someone great, you might become someone great, too. But our grandparents couldn't pronounce it, so he got stuck with Googi instead, and he used Guggenheim only for special occasions like graduation or confirmation, any moment he believed would change his life.

"So you're going to punch Paul McCartney, then ask him for an autograph," I said.

Googi gave me a look like I was the slow one. "We want to *meet* them, not *beat* them," he whispered.

"This is the Beatles we're talking about," JohnJohn said. "Don't act like you're on Uncle Willie's side."

Googi nodded. "Do you think John would sing 'It's Only Love' to me if I asked?" he asked.

JohnJohn socked him in the arm. "Don't be a queer."

"You can't ask for autographs, you can't ask for songs," I told them. "That isn't why we're doing this. We have a job to do, right?"

"For who?" JohnJohn said. "Imelda Marcos?" He lit the last cigarette from his pack, then took a long, deep drag like he was trying to breathe in and contain his anger. He was a copy editor at his school newspaper; the week before he'd worked on an article about the workers who died from heat-stroke while building a Mount Rushmore–sized monument of the President, which the First Lady demanded be finished despite the record heat. He showed me another article about a peasant village she had bulldozed in order to clear space for a nightclub that was never built, and when they protested, two villagers were shot. "Signs of things to come," he'd said.

He turned the framed picture of Imelda Marcos over, then mashed his cigarette against it, leaving glowing ashes on the glass. They looked like fireflies dancing around her, which made her look like some sort of fairy-tale queen, friend to all creatures great and small. I flicked them off with my finger.

"Filipina womanhood, my ass," he said, shuffling the cards.

"Just one song, that's all," Googi whispered to himself, still rubbing his arm where JohnJohn had hit him.

A light was still on in Uncle Willie's room. "Just deal," I said.

· · ·

IN LESS THAN AN HOUR JohnJohn and Googi were giggling drunks, and they had all my money. I was tired of letting them cheat, so I finished my beer and got up from the table, a little more than tipsy, and went to check on my uncle.

He always called it the second floor, but his bedroom was just three steps up from the back of the kitchen. Despite his good pay, he lived modestly—he never bought a house, and he'd rented that small one-bedroom apartment for as long as I'd been alive. "I like my things to be close together," he once said. I stood at the bottom step, watching him through the hanging strands of beads in the doorway as he ironed his work clothes for the next day. Behind him, Imelda Marcos was everywhere—pictures and articles tacked and taped on the wall, headlines that read IMELDA TAKES PARIS BY STORM and IMELDA LOVES AMERICA, AMERICA LOVES IMELDA. It was like a page from a giant scrapbook, full of airbrushed eight-by-tens and photos carefully torn from glossy magazines. But the wall was only half-covered, as though the other half was a reserved plot for the rest of Imelda's life. I imagined the empty space covered over with articles about Uncle Willie's victory against the Beatles, and an accompanying photo of him, arm in a sling and face bruised black and blue. A soldier smiling after the battle, despite the hurt.

"Still awake?" I said, to let him know I was there.

"You should be in bed."

"So should you."

"I'm old. I don't need sleep. But you're still growing."

He warned me about staying up too late, that nighttime drinking and gambling weren't the habits of an admirable man. "My sister would not approve," he said, and I suddenly pictured my mother on her Vacation USA, lying on a chaise lounge with cucumbers over her eyes and a towel turbaned on her head. I wondered what she pictured when she thought of me back here, if the image made her long for me, or simply feel relieved that she was gone.

"I'm not a kid," I said. "I don't need her approval."

Uncle Willie shook his head and sighed, then told me to come in.

I sat at the foot of his bed. Uncle Willie unplugged the iron, then slipped the shirt into an armor-gray blazer hanging on the closet door. Instead of the black tie he normally wore for work, he pulled from the top drawer a handful of ties I never knew he owned, and one by one he held them to the collar of his shirt, waiting for the right match. "Tomorrow is a special day," he said, "we must look our best." I'd never seen Uncle Willie fuss over his appearance like this, and he'd been a bachelor all his life. But as I watched him testing tie after tie, when I saw a newly opened bottle of cologne on top of his dresser, I wondered if he was trying to end that. I could smell Uncle Willie, the change in his scent. It was on his clothes, his skin, the air around us. I was only sixteen, but I thought that this might be love, that if something could change you so much, then maybe, in the end, it was worth fighting for, even if you weren't going to be loved back.

He reached for another tie but set it down, laughed at himself like he was being silly. "Simple is best," he decided. He looped the black tie around the collar.

"No. This one works better." I got up and took it away, replaced it with a turquoise tie patterned with silver paisley. "It goes with the gray."

Uncle Willie took a step back, sat on the edge of his bed and bent over, wiping away a bit of dust from his shoe. He stayed that way for a moment, then sat up and looked straight at me. "Do you think I'm crazy?" he asked.

It was the kind of question you ask only to see if the answer you get is the one you're hoping for. But Uncle Willie's face was blank; I really don't think he knew what the answer was at all, and whatever I said he would take as the truth.

"I think you're dutiful" was what I finally told him. He didn't know what the word meant. "Dutiful," I repeated. "It's like the knight who enters a battle without asking why." This was the best definition I could give. The answer seemed to please him.

"I'm honored to enter the battle," he said, "after all she has done for our country." Because of Imelda Marcos, he said, the world looked at us differently. "She dazzles and inspires. Who of us is able to do that?" He said that no matter how famous Imelda Marcos became, no matter how many times she flew off into the world, she always returned, always grateful to touch native ground. "She belongs to us." His voice was breaking; I could hear it. "It is our duty as men to protect her good name."

I looked past him, at an autographed photo of Imelda beside his bed. *For Willy,* she misspelled, *Love and Beauty, Imelda.* "It's getting late," I said. I told him good night and left through the hanging beads. At the bottom step I turned around, and I saw him kiss his finger, then press it against her picture; not on the lips or on the cheek—that wouldn't be appropriate for someone of his station—but on a spot near her shoulder, just above her heart. That part of her was sore, Uncle Willie once read, from all the corsages that had been pinned there during her travels abroad. "You see what she does for us?" he'd said. "It aches her to leave us, even for just a short while."

Then from behind me a clumsy two-part harmony started up. *"You're gonna lose that girl,"* my drunk cousins crooned to Uncle Willie, *"yes, yes, you're gonna loooose that giiirrl."*

"Leave him alone," I said, pushing them back into the living room. "He's fine."

THE SAN MIGUELS HIT MY cousins hard; JohnJohn was passed out on the couch, snoring and wheezing with every breath, and Googi was on the recliner, mumbling as he dreamed. Above, the ceiling fan creaked slowly, and I lay on the floor with a pillow over my head, trying to drown out the noise. I didn't know any tricks to help me fall asleep, so I tried going over Uncle Willie's plan of attack step by step, the who-what-where-and-when of it all, but before I could hear his voice or see his face I imagined my own, and zoomed ahead to tomorrow, to that moment when I would meet the Beatles. We would stand together—John and Paul to my left, Ringo and George to my right—chatting and laughing the way new friends do. Someone would take a picture, and later I'd give copies to my classmates and teachers, mail some to the local papers, and frame one for myself, a thing I'd keep forever. But the original I'd send to my mother, with a note written on the back that said *Look at me now.* She hadn't seen a picture of me since I was twelve, and my changed face would startle her, make her wonder about the life she was missing, and fill her with regret.

My moment with the Beatles was clear; I could see it perfectly. What I didn't understand was how the battle against them would lead up to it, if the fight was meant to happen immediately after, or how we could go from being new friends to new enemies, or vice versa. And the greater mystery was where Uncle Willie would be when the picture was taken, if he was nearby and ready to strike, or somewhere else entirely, a place I didn't know. I thought I'd lie awake forever trying to figure it out.

THE NEXT DAY, THE PARKING lot of Manila International Airport looked like a political protest: high above the crowds were banners and signs, and all you could hear was the noisy overlap of shouting voices. As our taxi pulled up to the curb, I thought that maybe Uncle Willie was right, that the Beatles really had said something so unforgivable to bring all these people together. But when I stepped out I understood what they were saying: BEATLES WE LOVE YOU and BEATLES COME BACK were painted in block letters on banners and posters, and weeping teenage girls screamed the same message. A line of arm-linked policemen could barely hold them back.

JohnJohn and I walked toward the entrance, but Googi turned to face the crowd. He threw his arms in the air and blew kisses, like they were gathered there for him. "I'm bigger than the Beatles!" he said. JohnJohn grabbed his arm, pulled him along.

Uncle Willie flashed his ID to security. "They are with me," he told the guard, gesturing to the three of us. He'd given us security blazers and fake name tags before we left his apartment, and they'd seemed convincing enough when we put them on, but now, standing in the terminal, we looked like kids playing dress-up. Still, the guard let us through.

We walked past the duty-free gift shops, the airport bar, the departing gates. At the end of the terminal, Uncle Willie reached for his keys and unlocked a door that read AIRPORT SECURITY ONLY, and we stepped into a long white corridor. We walked single file, Uncle Willie, Googi, JohnJohn, then me, all of us silent. I looked back at the white emptiness behind me, and I had the feeling that the farther we went in, the more impossible it would be to get back. "Almost there," Uncle Willie said.

He unlocked another door. We walked through and saw an escalator that led to Gate VIP, but before we went up, Uncle Willie gathered us together, and told us this was a momentous occasion, the first step in becoming truly honorable men. Then he opened his briefcase and pulled out a copy of *The Quotable Imelda: Famous Quotes from Imelda Marcos*. It had been required reading my freshman year in high school, an assignment I'd skipped, but Uncle Willie's copy was full of dog-eared pages, and the cover was tattered at the edges, like it was a beloved book he'd read over and over. "Listen to this," he said, opening to a bookmarked page, "and let her words inspire you." He cleared his throat, and began to read. *"The truth is that life is so beautiful and life is so prosperous and life is so full of potential and life has so much good in it, that I get bored and tired with ugliness, with negativism and evil and all of that. I start in the morning and I feel that we all have one thousand energy. In my case, I see a beautiful flower, a beautiful person, a beautiful smile, by that time I'm just about ready to take off! I have one million energy, no longer one thousand! This is why we are a beautiful people, a people with love, and so we must live our lives in the name of beauty and love."*

He closed the book. "Think about it," he said.

I looked at JohnJohn, and all I wanted was for him to laugh, to make a joke about the First Lady, anything to break the stone look on his face that stays with me even now.

"This isn't about her," I whispered.

"Then who?" he said. Before I could answer, he started up the escalator, Googi right behind him.

Uncle Willie was about to go up, but I grabbed his arm and held him back. "What if we lose?" I asked.

He blinked twice, like the question made no sense at all, so I repeated it, and followed it with more—what if the Beatles defeated us, and refused to apologize for what they'd said about the First Lady? What if the police arrived and threw us in jail? He could end up fired, and what good would he be to Imelda Marcos then? With every question I knew I might be sacrificing my only chance to meet the Beatles, which would be one of the great regrets of my life, but this was my last chance to save Uncle Willie, so I had to keep going. "We could lose," I said.

"With you at my side?" He gently removed my hand from his arm. "Impossible." He stepped onto the escalator, and I watched him rise up away from me, then step off at the top. Finally, I followed.

Gate VIP was a small square room furnished with a couch and two wing chairs, a Victorian-style coffee table in the center. To the side was a fireplace that didn't look quite real, and above it was a painting of a life-size Imelda Marcos, her head slightly tilted, her arms reaching out. "Run!" Googi whispered to me. "Before she destroys us with her one million energy!" I told him to shut up, but it really did look like those Imelda-arms were out to pull us into her, either to cradle or strangle us to death.

Uncle Willie called us to attention and reviewed the plan once more. As soon as the Beatles arrived, he would escort them to Gate VIP and have them proceed up the escalator.

The three of us would begin the attack while Uncle Willie and his own security team detained the group's bodyguards. "And then finally, I will join you up here to crush the Beatles," he said. My cousins nodded as if they were with him each step of the way, but I was fixed on the mess of paisley knotted at his throat, how wrong it looked in the daylight, and his cologne smelled sour and sharp, like vinegar mixed with rubbing alcohol.

"But who are we?" I asked. "What are we supposed to be doing when they arrive?"

"Just act like you're supposed to be here," Uncle Willie said, pointing to my name tag, "as if you belong." Then he shook each of our hands, wished us luck, and left.

Standing there alone with my cousins in a room meant only for the most important travelers in the world, I believed I was answering a call of duty. I kept my fists clenched and my head up, ready for the fight, but all we had on us was pen and paper for autographs, a camera hidden in Googi's pants pocket, and "Ticket to Ride" boomed inside my head.

WHEN I WAS A KID, Uncle Willie would bring me to the airport, and show it off like it was his. "You see all those people leaving and returning?" he said on my first visit. "I am the one who is responsible for them."

"Where do they go?" I asked. I was seven, maybe eight years old.

"That way," he pointed skyward, then moved his hand

to the side. "Then that way." I always assumed he meant to the States.

Uncle Willie lifted me up, brought me close to the window overlooking the tarmac. The glass felt hot against my forehead, and I could feel the vibrations of the planes' revving engines. But when their wheels left the ground, I had to look away; I couldn't believe that something so big and heavy could stay afloat in the air. I thought of emergency landings, of airplanes bobbing in the middle of the ocean, all the crashes I'd seen on the news. "Will you go, too?" I asked.

Uncle Willie shook his head, promising me that he wasn't going anywhere, that his job was to stay behind to make sure everything ran just right. I loved him for that. Growing up, I watched branches of my family break off as they headed to the States, aunts and uncles taking my cousins with them. For years my mother watched her sisters pack as soon as their husbands' requests for transfer went through, and fighting with my father was how she dealt with being left. *I'm stuck here*, she would say. *Why didn't you join the service like the rest of the men? Where is your ambition? Don't you at least want your son to be somebody?* My mother stood behind me when she said this, cupping my shoulders with her hands, presenting me as an example of my father's failure. He looked at me apologetically, but he never said a word.

The year I turned twelve, she finally got to go. Her younger sister sent her a ticket with a small note attached that said *For your VACATION USA!* and my mother started packing that same day. Tourist visa only, she assured me the morning she left. I wanted to see her off at the gate, but a sign read NO WELL-WISHERS BEYOND THIS POINT, and the guard refused to let me pass. I wanted to tell him that the sign didn't apply to me, that I didn't wish my mother well at all, that in fact, I wished her a terrible trip, a time so awful she would take the first flight back to Manila. But my father reassured me that tourists couldn't be gone forever, that she had no choice but to come home. I took that technicality as my guarantee for her return, but six months later, on the back of a postcard of the Golden Gate Bridge, I learned that the visa had become a green card. *The weather is good for my health, for my skin,* she wrote. *You should see how well I look.* My father gave it a glance, said, "Her life," and handed it back to me, then left to play mah-jongg at the corner cantina. Uncle Willie was there, and he told me not to worry. "She's away," he said, "for now." But that was just another version of the truth, an easier way of saying, *She left us.*

I thought leaving was a terrible thing, the saddest of acts, something you do to the people you love.

But in junior high school, Uncle Willie got me a part-time job at the airport helping passengers with their bags. While I dragged and pushed along heavy luggage, they would walk ahead of me, fanning themselves with their tickets like they were flaunting their travels. I never checked their destinations; all I knew was that they were leaving for someplace far away, and that their eventual return would be a triumphant one, like astronauts coming back from outer space. I daydreamed myself into those airport reunions I witnessed throughout the day: I would get off the plane and find my family waiting, their arms spread out in welcome, my cousins asking question after question, everyone impressed by the way I'd changed.

When I finally took a monthlong trip to visit my mother in California for my fourteenth birthday, my homecoming was a disappointment. Only Uncle Willie was waiting for me at the airport, and all he asked about was my return flight, whether or not the service was satisfactory, if I was able to sleep away the long hours to make the trip feel quicker than it was. "It's good that you are back," he said, loading my bags into the trunk of a taxi. He paid the driver and told him to take me home. I rolled the windows down, and the backseat filled with a mugginess I hadn't really noticed before. It clung to me, and all I wanted was to feel cool again, the way I did in California. When I got home, no one was there; my father was out, and JohnJohn and Googi didn't collect their souvenir T-shirts until the following afternoon. For the next month, I slept through the day and paced the house at night, restless and sweaty, my body and mind still on American time. Back then I thought it was the seventeen-hour difference that inverted my days. Two years later, in that moment when Googi tapped me on the shoulder and twice whispered, "The Beatles are coming," into my ear, I knew that jetlag had had nothing to do with my ruined sleep.

.   .   .

WE HEARD VOICES BELOW. FROM above we watched
Uncle Willie direct the Beatles toward the escalator. As
planned, there were no porters to assist them with their luggage, and I heard Paul complain about the weight of his
bags. "Porter shortage in the Philippines?" he said.

"No porter?" Ringo asked. "I'll take whatever's on draft,
then."

Uncle Willie hurried them along. As soon as each Beatle
was on his way, he looked at us and nodded. *It's up to you
now* was what I read in his face, so I shut my eyes, trying
to remember the plans he drew on the tabletop the night
before, the *X*'s and arrows indicating who and where we
were meant to be. But all I could picture was Uncle Willie's
reflection in the glass, shadowy on one side, full of light on
the other; there one moment, gone the next.

Then the Beatles finally came. Before that day, I'd known
them only as a single sound of blended voices among gui-
tar riffs and drumbeats. I would play their records and
watch the needle curve along the grooves, then try to work
my own voice into their harmonies. I always sang in secret,
embarrassed by my voice; when no one was in the house
I would sit on the floor next to the stereo speakers, belt-
ing out their lyrics like they were truths about myself. And
now they were here, and they were real, entering my life
one by one as the escalator steps rose and vanished into
the floor: Ringo, then Paul, then George, and finally John,
who was holding a Super 8 movie camera, and filming
every moment. Each Beatle was dressed in bright, loose-

fitting shirts that seemed to change color with the slightest movement, and when they stepped closer, I saw that their skin was the same way. Their white English faces were unexpectedly tanned, pink in the cheeks and red at the ears from the Philippine sun. It was a sign of their travels, evidence of a bigger world, proof that you could move through it and keep it with you. I remember standing there by that fake fireplace between my cousins in our borrowed blazers and fake name tags, thinking, *This is it. This is the real thing. This is what it means to be in the world.*

Ringo was the first to speak to us. "There's no porter shortage at all," he said.

"No, but shorter porters they are," Paul said, tapping each of us on the head. "But you can take these onto the plane if you don't mind." He dropped his carry-on luggage to the floor. The other Beatles did the same.

JohnJohn picked up two bags. I followed his lead. But Googi just stood there, sweaty and pale. He was almost reverent in the way he looked at Paul, and he kept swallowing, like he wanted to speak. "My name is—" he finally said, but he was so nervous he mispronounced it.

"Huggengeim?" George said, one eyebrow raised. "Type of cheese, isn't it? All the same, nice ring to it."

"Thank you." Googi was beaming.

"Anything to say to the camera?" Paul asked. He looked back at John, whose face was hidden behind the lens, which was now pointed at us. "Go on, lads. Whatever you like." My cousins and I looked at each other, as if someone was supposed to cue someone else, give him the right words to say. But none of us could speak.

"Come on, man," Paul said. "Just give a shout. Wave hello. Anything at all."

I could hear the camera rolling, the filmed moments passing by. I had no idea if these were the Beatles' home movies, something they'd watch again whenever they wanted to reminisce, or if it was for the whole world to see, a way of bringing them along as the Beatles traveled the globe. Our silence continued, so I thought of the things people said whenever they were caught on camera—bystanders on the TV news, or athletes in the first post-victory moments. *Hi Mom.* That was it. So I stepped forward and said it too, straight into the lens. I even waved, as if she could truly see me. My cousins did the same, and the three of us laughed nervously at ourselves. The Beatles started laughing too, and now we all laughed together, like we'd been chums for years. I said nothing else, never even told them my name, but it didn't matter. JohnJohn looked truly happy for the first time in months, and even now I'm sure there were joyful tears welling in Googi's eyes. I wanted to plant myself there, take root in that moment with the Beatles and my cousins, and never leave it, not ever.

Quick as it was, the picture of it is clearer to me now: the Beatles in a line, facing my cousins and me, a four-on-three standoff that should commence into battle. But what Uncle Willie finds when he reaches the top of the escalator is a friendly exchange between his enemy and his allies, a truce he never called. And when I turn to look at him I'm just stuck, like someone ankle-deep in hardening mud, and I can't run or hide or change my traitorous face. I betrayed my uncle, and the woman he loved.

So I acted.

"Now!" I said. I stepped away from the group, then pushed a potted plant over, hoping it would crash upon a Beatle like a fallen tree, pinning him to the ground. But it just landed softly on a wing chair and dirt spilled everywhere, soiling Paul's and Ringo's shoes. I kept going, throwing their bags across the room and into the fake fireplace, and Uncle Willie nodded, like everything was going according to plan after all, and he stepped forward, too. I picked up another carry-on, hurling it onto the down escalator. *Take that, Beatles!* was the intended message, but it fell like a tumbleweed, and George said, "That's my bag," and Paul said, "He wanted to check that." I ignored them both, and took the gift basket of mangoes at Ringo's feet and kicked it over, the fruit rolling onto the floor, and I picked them up and threw them hard against the ground like grenades. All the while, Googi struggled to work the flash on his camera, and JohnJohn took fast, nervous drags of his cigarette, looking confused in a corner of the room. "Don't just stand there," I said, but as soon as I ran out of things to knock over and throw, all I could do was remove myself from the scene, too.

But Uncle Willie wouldn't stop, and soon he had John by the collar. "So *you* are the rascals who are more popular than Jesus Christ," he said. John nodded, the camera still in his hand, and Uncle Willie tried shaking him into submission. He was near tears about Imelda, almost incoherent, and what I saw next was his hand curl into a fist and John's camera drop to the ground, the film popping out, my hello to the world overexposed, gone forever.

Suddenly a dozen other bodies rushed up the escalator, and they looked like real airport security guards. "Come on, everybody," Uncle Willie shouted, "for Imelda!" "For Imelda!" they shouted back, and the mob closed in. I didn't know if Uncle Willie had planned this from the start, if he recruited true Marcos loyalists because he knew we would fail him in the end. I called his name, fighting through the crowd to reach him, but when I touched his shoulder he swiped my arm away and told me to leave him alone, to get out, to go. Then someone shoved me, and I fell backwards to the ground. Next to my hand was a mango, so I picked it up and threw it hard against the painting of Imelda Marcos, hitting her in the center of her chest. An orange, pulpy ooze bloomed like a flower, then dripped down like blood. I wanted to call out to Uncle Willie, to show him what I had done, but my cousins grabbed me, pulling me toward the escalator. "It's over," JohnJohn said, "let's go!" We ran down, and all I saw when I looked back was my uncle vanish in the haze, his war cry in the name of love drowned out by all the Imeldamania.

We ran through the corridor and headed for the entrance. "What about Uncle Willie?" I said, and my cousins said to forget him, that there was nothing we could do. I kept running, sweating in the thick polyester blazer, the name tag flopping up and down against my chest. I finally stopped at the long line of policemen trying to contain the thousands of fans who cried out, "Beatles, don't leave us, Beatles, don't go."

In the end, airport police broke up the fight, which lasted only minutes after we fled the scene. No arrests were made and the Beatles made it to their plane, none of them seriously injured, but they never came our way again.

"YES," GOOGI TOLD REPORTERS, "I witnessed the whole thing." We ended up making the papers, the international news, and for the first time the world came to us, calling late at night, knocking on our doors early in the morning for interviews. Googi basked in his brief fame, and JohnJohn tried to use the spotlight to expose the corruption in the Marcos government, but reporters just stopped their tape recorders and put down their pens when he spoke. I stayed quiet, letting everyone else remember and tell the story however they wanted.

But Uncle Willie made his role in the attack known, and what he got in the end was a reprimand from the President himself. And Imelda Marcos—essence of Filipina woman-hood, face of our country—called the incident a breach of Filipino hospitality, and she offered more quotable wisdom to help the people understand what had happened. "In life, ugliness must sometimes occur," she said. "But when such ugliness happens, only beauty can arrive, 'to save the day,' so to speak. Despite the ugly events of the past days, beauty has returned, so let's focus only on the beautiful things and let beauty live on." Ashamed for any embarrassment he brought to the First Lady, Uncle Willie issued an official apology, and resigned soon after.

But he didn't disappear. "I still have one million energy," he said. He took a job as an airport shuttle driver, carting tourists to nearby hotels, and on his lunch break he'd hang around the terminal, making sure Imelda Marcos's flights were on schedule, and offering unwanted advice on how best to handle her travels. "They say I am a pest, but I know they still need me," he said. "Imelda still needs me."

Years later, after I joined my mother in California, I made a final trip to the Philippines. Googi had run off to Hong Kong with an English businessman years before, and JohnJohn was dead, one of the few to take a Marcos bullet in the People Power Revolution of '86. But when I walked into Uncle Willie's apartment, everything felt the same: the ceiling fan still creaked when it turned, beads hung in the doorway, and there was a case of San Miguel in the refrigerator. The only difference was that Imelda Marcos's presence had grown. There were more stories and pictures crowding his bedroom wall, some of them recent, as if she were still the First Lady.

We did very little that week; Uncle Willie was eighty years old, and all he wanted to do was nap or watch television.

But late one night, he told me he had something to show me, and he put a videocassette into the VCR. "Watch," he said, then pressed the PLAY button. The screen went blue, and suddenly the Beatles appeared on the screen, doing an interview in which they mentioned the incident. "Do you remember the battle?" Uncle Willie asked from his wheelchair. "How bravely we fought?" I smiled and told him I could never forget.

I turned up the volume. "I hated the Philippines," Ringo said bluntly. George and John agreed, smoking before the cameras, but Paul was more introspective. "It was one of those places where you knew they were waiting for a fight," he said. Uncle Willie nodded, confirming its truth. I stared at the Beatles' faces, and I wondered if they remembered mine, if they would know who I was if they saw me now.

"If I had become an American, like you," Uncle Willie said, "I would have been knighted." I didn't tell him that they do that only in England. In America, you might get a compliment in the papers, maybe a medal for bravery, but nothing that big. You would be the same person as when you started, long before the fight. That much I'd come to know. Still, I told him yes, that most certainly he would have been knighted, and I proceeded to create for him a picture of the ceremony, of Uncle Willie on his knee and Imelda on her throne, a sword in her hand, its blade gentle on his shoulder.

Save the I-Hotel

———

THE HUMAN BARRICADE SURROUNDING THE INTER-
national Hotel was six deep, two thousand arm-linked protestors chanting, *We won't go! Save the I-Hotel!* Inside, dozens more
crammed the halls, blocking the stairwell with mattresses,
desks, their own bodies. But it was past midnight now, fire
engines blocked both ends of Kearny Street, and police in
riot gear were closing in, armed with batons and shields.

"I hate this street," Vicente said.

"It's nothing," Fortunado said. He stood at the window
watching the protest below, his fingers between the slats of
the blinds. "Just traffic."

"I'm telling you, it's the Chinese again. Their parade
always clogging the city." He sat on the edge of his bed,
folding a thin gray sweater over his lap. They were in his
room on the third floor of the I-Hotel, next door to Fortunado's. "Don't worry, Nado. We'll make it through."

Fortunado closed the blinds, wiped the dust from his fingers. "We will," he said.

The threat of eviction had loomed for more than a decade, and now it was happening. The mayor of San Francisco had approved the hotel's demolition and ordered the removal of its final tenants, the elderly Filipino men who had lived in the I-Hotel for more than forty years. Earlier that day, protest organizers had gathered the tenants in the lobby to prepare them for the fight, and told them to stay in their rooms until the very end. "But pack a bag," they said, "just in case." After, Fortunado hurried upstairs, woke Vicente from a nap, and though he meant to tell him about the eviction, he told him they were taking a weekend trip instead, just the two of them. He hadn't named a specific place, but Vicente was easy to persuade. These days, he barely recognized the world as it was: he never knew the day or time, his oldest friends were strangers, and just three weeks before, Fortunado found him on the corner of Kearny Street and Columbus, only a block from the entrance of the I-Hotel, asking strangers to help him find his way home. Now, the shouting in the halls and the sirens on the street were simply the ruckus of a Chinese New Year in his mind. He knew nothing of an eviction, had no sense of a coming end.

Vicente's hands shook as he folded another sweater. Distant sirens drew closer. Fortunado thought, *This is what it means to be old*. Now, he wished youth back, and if granted, he would offer it up to Vicente, who would make better use of it. He imagined Vicente springing to his feet and running down the stairs to claim his place in the barricade, his fists raised and ready to defend their right to stay. He was, Fortunado always knew, the stronger one.

IT WAS AUGUST 4, 1977. They had lived in the I-Hotel for forty-three years.

They never meant to stay so long.

They met on a September night in 1934. Fortunado had been in the States for five months, working fifteen-hour days in the asparagus fields just outside Stockton; this trip to San Francisco was his first chance to get away. He stepped off a Greyhound bus at the end of Market Street and wandered the grid of downtown, unable to distinguish the places that welcomed Filipinos from those that refused them. It was dark when he finally spotted a trio of Filipino men smoking cigarettes outside a barely lit doorway, and though no one said hello, they stepped aside to let him through.

He entered a long, narrow dance hall filled with mixed couples, Filipino men with white women. A gray-bearded man with a cane circled the room, calling out, "Dime a ticket, ticket a dance," and in the corner, a half dozen women sat in metal chairs, waiting for the next customer. A banner that read *Welcome to the Dreamland Saloon* sagged on the wall above them.

Fortunado bought three tickets, moved closer to the dance floor. He watched the couple closest to him. The man danced with his eyes closed, whispering into the woman's ear; the woman yawned, then scratched something from her teeth.

Fortunado put the tickets in his pocket and took a chair by the wall. This would be a night of music to enjoy alone, nothing more, and it would be enough.

A new song began, and a man with a beer in each hand stomped across the dance floor, pestering girls for free dances. "Sorry, Vicente," a girl with a long cigarette said, "no money, no honey." She blew smoke in his face and walked off. "Your loss," Vicente shouted back. He finished one beer, then the other. He was tall for a Filipino, lanky in his fitted blazer and trousers. He zigzagged through the crowd, bumping into couples, then suddenly tripped over the ticket man's cane. "I'm fine, everybody," Vicente shouted, gaining his balance, "I'm just fine," and to prove it he began dancing alone, swaying side to side with some imaginary partner. He was a drunk, pathetic sight but Fortunado couldn't help but laugh.

Vicente saw him and walked over. "If I'm so funny," he said, wiping his mouth with the back of his sleeve, "then where's your girl, big shot?"

Fortunado shrugged.

"With all these fine girls around? Your head must be broken." Vicente flicked Fortunado's forehead twice, like he was checking the ripeness of a coconut. Fortunado swiped his arm away, and warm beer came spilling over Fortunado's head.

"Idiot!" Fortunado got to his feet. "You want to dance so badly? Then take them." He took the tickets from his pocket and threw them to the floor, shoved Vicente aside, and walked off.

In the washroom, he ran a red cocktail napkin under warm water, wiped his head and dabbed the beer from his shirt, the lapel of his jacket. He thought of his life in America: the hot, dusty hours in the fields, the muggy nights in the bunkhouses, all the workers who passed the time regretting the new life and lamenting the old. They were new arrivals too, most of them Filipinos, and they never stopped telling him: *Nobody knows you here, just the work you do, just the color of your face.* They called America a mistake, and now the dream was to find a way back home, to the life you knew and the person you were. Tonight was meant to prove that he had been right to come.

He looked in the mirror. The shoulders of his borrowed blazer were wider than his own. The sleeves fell past his knuckles. *Fool,* he thought to himself.

The door opened and he saw Vicente in the edge of the mirror. "Never pay for dances," he said, setting the tickets on the sink. "That way, you find out which girls want your dimes and which ones really want to dance with you." He reached for Fortunado's lapel. "Messy boy. Wear mine." He removed his jacket and held it out, a peace offering.

"I'm fine with my own."

"Suit yourself." He lit a cigarette, introduced himself, then asked, "What's your name?" a question Fortunado had not heard since he was hired in the fields five months before. In his life now, weeks could pass without ever hearing his name.

So he told him.

"Fortunado." Vicente shook his head, exhaling smoke. "Too long. I'll call you Nado." He stamped out his cigarette on the wet, crumpled napkin and stepped toward the door. "This place is dead, Nado. Let's move on." He held the door open, and though Fortunado didn't move, Vicente continued to stand there, waiting. Fortunado realized that Vicente had come to the Dreamland alone too.

They walked up and down the streets and Vicente named them: Kearny, Washington, Jackson, Clay. Certain blocks felt more familiar than the rest, those lined with small eateries and shops named Bataan Kitchen, the Manila Rose Cantina, the Lucky Mabuhay Pool Hall. All around, Filipino men smoked, laughed, and drank from silver flasks, hollering for each other and darting across the street, as if this city had been theirs from the beginning. And sitting on the top step of an apartment building was the oldest Filipino Fortunado had ever seen in America, gazing at the moon as if it held the face of the one he loved.

"Manilatown," Vicente said. "Our small place in San Francisco. Just like home, eh?"

Fortunado shook his head. This was better.

They continued walking, and Vicente told his story: he came here alone from Manila at the start of '33, scrubbed toilets and floors for a miserable half-year before finding better work as a bellhop in the Parkdale Hotel, a decent job with barely decent pay, but the best you could do in times like these. "It's hard out here, sometimes," he said, slowing his pace, "you get lonely, you get scared . . ." His voice trailed off as though these were his final words for the night, the truth he finally had to admit. But then he stopped, turned to Fortunado. "So be tough, okay?" He smiled, then punched Fortunado gently on the arm.

Hours passed, bars and restaurants closed. They found themselves at the end of the city, and walked along the Embarcadero. "Look there," Vicente said, pointing toward the water, and through the dark Fortunado saw it: the beginnings of the Bay Bridge. It would be the longest steel structure in the world, eight miles connecting San Francisco to Oakland. For now, it was only a line of towers rising from the black water, half-hidden in fog, and Fortunado wondered when it would be finished, if someday he might travel across it.

"I don't want to go back," he said.

"Then don't," Vicente said. "What's in Stockton anyway?"

Nothing. Just the hard, thin mattress Fortunado slept on, the canvas bag filled with the few clothes he owned, and more days in the fields with the kind of men he dreaded becoming.

They made their way to 848 Kearny Street and entered the I-Hotel, where Vicente kept a room for six dollars a week. He offered his floor for the night and Fortunado accepted, rolled up his coat for a pillow and used Vicente's as a blanket. It was his best sleep in America yet. The next day, Vicente loaned Fortunado twelve dollars for two weeks' rent, and he checked into number 14 on the third floor, the room next door to Vicente's and exactly the same: a small, narrow space with a twin bed, a corner sink, a three-drawer bureau, and a single window that looked out on the 800 block of Kearny Street. Below, Fortunado could see two Filipino groceries, a barbershop, a Chinese laundry, and on the rooftop across, an unfinished billboard with a half-painted picture of a crate of apples, the word *new* written in yellow letters beneath.

"Not much of a view," Vicente said.

Fortunado opened the window, letting in a breeze. "Good enough for now," he said.

FORTUNADO WAS TWENTY YEARS OLD that night they met. Vicente was twenty-four.

Now, Fortunado was sixty-three. Vicente, sixty-seven.

Neither of them married. No one in the I-Hotel ever did, and when they wanted to, the law forbade them. No Filipino could bring a wife or fiancée to the States back then, and there were no Filipinas here. Marrying white women, even dating them, was illegal, and always dangerous. The same week he arrived in California, a Filipino field worker was beaten to death for swimming in a lake with his white girlfriend.

The law changed in 1967. "I've been alone this long," Vicente had said, "what would I do with a wife?" He was fifty-seven by then, too old and too late to bother with marriage. "She'd want a bigger place, something expensive. No thanks, I'm fine where I am." But during their Saturday afternoon walks through Chinatown, the sight of a wedding banquet in a Chinese restaurant made him silent, suddenly tired and irritable. He would hurry back to the I-Hotel, pour himself a shot of Du Kang, the gold-colored Chinese liquor they drank as young men, and pace the short distance of his room as though trapped inside it, then finally sit at the window with his hands on the sill, staring down at the slow-moving traffic. From the sidewalk below, Fortunado would watch him, knowing Vicente's regrets—the years of come-and-go women, the time and money wasted on prostitutes, the better life he might have lived had he been brave enough to try. And Fortunado would think, *I'm sorry*.

Somewhere close, glass shattered. Vicente looked up from his packing, turned toward the door as if to investigate, then brushed his knuckles against his jaw. "I want to shave before we leave," he said. He went to the sink and turned on the faucet, waited for cold water to turn hot.

Fortunado went to the door and looked through the peephole: protesters crammed more furniture into the stairwell, others hammered wood planks over windows already boarded up, and at the end of the hallway, three men chained themselves to exposed pipes running down the wall while the rest cheered them on.

Fortunado double-checked the locks, tugged at the knob, and made sure the door would hold. "It's just the parade," he said.

· · ·

FORTUNADO HAD LEFT STOCKTON WITH no money and no plan, but in the beginning, San Francisco worked the way America should: he had a friend, a room of his own, and soon after, a bellhop position at the Parkdale Hotel.

Vicente lied to get Fortunado the job: he told his boss that a cousin with three years' experience as the houseboy of Seattle's ex-mayor had just arrived in the city, looking for work. "I told them I've known you my whole life," he explained, "so try to act like it."

The following morning, they caught the first cable car on the California line, rode to the top of Nob Hill, and stepped off at Powell and Mason. Straight ahead was the Parkdale Hotel, seven stories high, twenty windows across, and from where Fortunado stood it seemed the rest of the city had vanished behind it. Inside, a dozen marble pillars held up the lobby's mahogany ceiling, a brass staircase spiraled upward, and in the copper elevator doors, Fortunado could see his reflection: his bellhop uniform fit tightly and made him stand up straight, his pomade-slicked hair gleamed under the light, and the dozen buttons on his coat could be mistaken for gold.

Those months in the fields stooped over in the dusty heat, the brim of his hat casting an unending shadow on his face—that was someone else's anonymous life. Now, when Fortunado crossed the lobby, he would welcome guests in his best English, and they, in turn, regarded him with courteous smiles. But the best times in the day, those moments when he believed he was where he belonged, were when he passed Vicente in the hallway or on the stairs: Vicente would nod with a quick smile of recognition, and sometimes, when no one was watching, he would reach out and punch Fortunado on the arm, just below his shoulder.

At the end of Fortunado's first month in the city, Vicente raised a bottle of Du Kang to the night sky and said, "To Nado, the finest houseboy in all of Seattle." He took a swig, and passed it over. Fortunado drank, swallowed slowly to ease the burn.

They were on the third-floor fire escape of the I-Hotel, too tired to change out of their uniforms. They sat for hours, laughing as they reminisced about the night they met, as though it had happened years instead of only weeks before. But as the night grew darker and colder, their faces turned serious, their voices quiet. "It's good that I found you," Vicente said, "finally someone I can talk to who doesn't whine about life."

"You can't listen," Fortunado said. "They'll get you down."

"But it's tough. No family. No wife. No home of my own." Vicente brought the bottle to his lips but didn't drink.

Fortunado put his hand on Vicente's shoulder. "Those things will happen. I promise."

"It's better here, yeah? We were right to come?"

Fortunado leaned in, so close he saw Vicente's eyes glisten, and said yes.

They let moments pass in silence, and a solitary car drove down Kearny. "I'm drunk," Vicente said, setting the bottle of Du Kang by Fortunado's feet. "What's left is yours." He rested his head against the brick wall, blinked slowly until his eyes stayed shut. He was shivering, so Fortunado took off his jacket and draped it over Vicente's shoulders, tucked it under his chin. His hands were just below his jaw; then a finger, at the edge of his lip. Fortunado had been this close with others before: those few flirtatious men back home, who at some point became willing. But it was never like this: below the street was empty and silent, every window and doorway was black, and the sliver of moon cast no light. These were signs that the world was offering up this moment, a chance to understand what it was like to kiss the one you knew, perhaps loved. *Good night,* he told himself, *that's all it means,* and moved closer until their faces touched. He kissed Vicente, and just as he was about to apologize, he felt Vicente kissing him too.

Then Vicente turned away. "It's late," he whispered, eyes still closed, "time to go back." He got to his feet and climbed through the window, and Fortunado watched him walk down to the far end of the hallway, where he unlocked his door and shut it behind him. It was almost light when Fortunado finally returned to his room. He sat on his bed with his back to the wall, listened to Vicente on the other side, breathing and turning in his sleep.

Later, just before work, Vicente opened Fortunado's door, already dressed in his uniform. "Come on, slowpoke," he said, snapping his fingers twice. He made no mention of the night before, only that his head still buzzed from the

Du Kang they shared. Then he hurried down the stairs and Fortunado slowly got up, and when he saw his face in the mirror above the sink, he understood how this would go: as it did back home—with silence and forgetting, the only way he knew.

All that became of their kiss was longing. Fortunado began counting off days and weeks since it happened, believing that enough passing time would blur the night into one that perhaps never happened at all. But it only brightened in his mind, and when months dragged into a year and then another, it was an absolute truth: once, long ago, they had kissed. On nights when Vicente caroused in bars with easy women or purchased hours in a Chinatown brothel, Fortunado would lie awake in bed, so restless that he kicked away his sheets, dressed, and walked down the empty blocks of Manilatown to the Embarcadero, where he would stand by the rail and look out at the Bay Bridge, which was nearly finished. Its progress was evidence that the world still turned forward, leaving behind a night when he was truly happy, and the moment he was utterly and finally known.

"I HATE THE BUS," VICENTE said, sorting through a pile of mismatched socks. "The seats hurt my back. No buses, Nado." He never wondered where they were going, only how they would get there.

"We won't take a bus," Fortunado said. He stood at

the dresser, gathering their California ID's, Social Security cards, and passports, then stuffed them into a yellow envelope, along with a letter from the West Oakland Senior Center, where tenants would be temporarily housed if the eviction happened. There was no plan beyond that; some might return to another San Francisco facility, others to Daly City or San Jose.

"Amtrak is faster. We'll take Amtrak, right?"

Fortunado sealed the envelope, wrote their names across the flap. "I've got the tickets," he said, "don't worry." He looked up at Vicente, and saw that he had shaved only the right side of his face. He was careless with his grooming these days: he might remember to change his undershirt but not his underwear or socks; when he showered, he would forget to rinse the soap from his body, then go through his day with white streaks of dry soap on his arms and neck. "You didn't finish," Fortunado said.

Vicente looked in the mirror above the sink, brushed his thumb against his cheek. Beneath the lightbulb above, his stubble look thorny and white, as though painful to touch.

"Here," Fortunado said, "I'll do it." He filled the sink with water, took out a disposable razor and shaving cream from the shoe box beneath. He lathered the left side of Vicente's face, wiped his hand dry, then stepped behind him.

"Don't cut me," Vicente said.

Fortunado shook his head. "I won't."

The sirens were much louder now, police shouted threats of arrest through their megaphones, but in the hall, the protesters continued: *Block the front door. Check the roof. Hurry.* But when Fortunado leaned in, he could hear the razor slide gently down Vicente's skin, the drops of water trickle from the faucet, and the night was quiet again. When he was younger, he had yearned for this closeness, ached for it, and now that Vicente could no longer care for himself, these were the necessary gestures of their everyday lives. And Fortunado welcomed the responsibility, secretly cherished it. Duty fulfilled desire, as best it could.

Vicente flinched. There was no blood; Fortunado had barely nicked the skin. But as Vicente wiped away the shaving cream from his face, Fortunado saw a spot of red, reflected in the corner of the mirror: the time on the digital clock, its numbers backwards and inverted, urgent and glowing. 12:03 A.M. The next day already, and Fortunado realized he hadn't packed a suitcase of his own.

1936. JUNE. TWO YEARS IN the city and nothing had changed. "What a life," Vicente said, passing a bottle of Du Kang to Fortunado. They were on the fire escape, exhausted from a double shift, and he was drunk. "Two hotels. One where I work. One where I live." Fortunado drank and passed the bottle back, but instead of drinking Vicente turned the bottle upside down and let the rest spill through the grate. "How can you stand it," he said, and climbed inside as if he didn't want to know the answer.

Then, only a day later, there was a girl.

Her name was Althea. Vicente was on the seventh floor of the Parkdale, hurrying to the elevator, when a maid called out, holding a gold button between her fingers. It had fallen from his blazer, and she insisted on sewing it on for him. "Guess where she fixed it," Vicente said to Fortunado later that night. "In the Berlin Deluxe." He spoke like he was bragging: the Berlin Deluxe was the hotel's grandest suite, but still under renovation after a room fire six months before. "She had a maid's key, and sometimes she goes there just to smoke a cigarette and look at the view. We sat by the window, for almost an hour. No one even saw us."

Except for the Berlin Deluxe, Fortunado had entered every guest room in the Parkdale, but just far enough to unload bags and luggage. He was never invited to look out the window, to gaze at the hotel's famous city views. "What was it like?" he asked.

Vicente looked at him and shook his head, as if what he saw was beyond Fortunado's imagination. "You could see everything," he said.

The following Sunday, coming home after another double shift, they saw Althea on Columbus Street. She was standing in front of a Chinese clothier, looking at the window display, a mannequin clad in black velvet, surrounded by boxes wrapped in silver paper. Behind it was a framed map of America, and Althea stared at it, as if studying all forty-eight states. "Planning a trip?" Vicente asked.

She turned toward them. Her red hair fell past her shoulders, and a lime-green scarf was tied loosely around her thin, pale neck; she was like no maid Fortunado had ever seen. "I'm just looking back at home, " she said, tapping her finger on the window. "Toward the middle, right there. Wisconsin. That's where I'm from. Mount Horeb. A tiny place."

"Do you miss it?" Vicente asked.

She shook her head. "Girls back there get married, have babies, and then they're stuck. If I'd stayed, that's what I would have become."

Vicente took a step forward. "And what are you now?"

She smiled playfully, as though Vicente had asked a trick question. "I'm new," she said. "Like you. Like everybody here." She took a small tin box of mints from her purse, and offered one to Vicente. "What about you," she said, "do you miss home?"

"I don't really think about it," he said, then took a mint. Only when Fortunado said hello did Vicente finally make proper introductions.

The sun had set but the night was still warm, so Althea suggested a cold beer at a nearby tavern on Fourth Street. They walked down Kearny, crossed over to Third, and below Market the sidewalks narrowed as the crowds thickened; Fortunado fell several steps behind but could still hear Althea talk about living in San Francisco, how quickly everything moved—the streetcars, the people, even time. But life dragged too: her boardinghouse room was stuffy and dim, the walls and single window unable to keep out any noise, barely a comfort after long shifts at the Parkdale.

"Sometimes I stay awake all night, no matter how tired I am," she said.

Vicente nodded. "I stay awake too." They walked so close their arms could touch.

Fortunado stopped, and as they moved farther down the block he recognized the slight zigzag in Vicente's step. It was the way he moved the night they met at the Dreamland, and now he recognized Althea too. She could be any Dreamland girl, but there was a difference: when Vicente looked at her, she looked back at him.

They were half a block ahead now. Fortunado decided to leave, to return to the I-Hotel or make his way to the Embarcadero, to its darkest, emptiest spot. But then a stocky, pink-faced man stepped out of a bar, his sleeves rolled up and shoes untied, and stumbled toward Vicente and Althea, raving about brown men taking white women and white jobs. He grabbed Vicente's shoulder and turned him around, put a finger in his chest. Vicente stepped back, tried walking away, but the man took him by the collar and shoved him against a storefront window. He threw a punch, and Vicente fell.

Fortunado ran to Vicente, fists clenched, ready to fight. But the man was too quick, too strong, and he grabbed Fortunado by the shoulder and pushed him to the ground. He heard his name—*Nado*—and when he looked up Vicente was back on his feet, punching the man in his stomach. "I'm not scared of you," he said, "I'm not scared." With every blow he said it, until Fortunado pulled him off.

They hurried back to the I-Hotel, ran up to Vicente's room. Fortunado went to the window, checking to see if they'd been followed. "We were just walking," he heard Althea say, "that's all." But he knew the truth, and saw it reflected in the glass: Vicente and Althea on the edge of the bed, his arm around her shoulder.

THE LAST THING LEFT OF Manilatown was the I-Hotel, and the human barricade was crumbling. Fortunado watched protesters fall to the batons of police, handcuffed and dragged away, and those still standing were not enough: a group of officers finally broke through, charged the front entrance with sledgehammers in hand. Behind him, Vicente slept atop the covers facing the wall, his coat and shoes already on.

In the hall, someone with a megaphone told tenants to keep their doors locked, block them with whatever they could move, so Fortunado went to the bureau, pushed it toward the door. But it was heavier than he thought, and he could feel his rushing heartbeat, the sweat on his face and neck. He stopped, took a breath, and just as he meant to try again he caught sight of something he had seen a thousand times before: the empty space on the floor beside Vicente's bed. Fortunado lay there once, and he remembered how well he had slept, how Vicente's coat had kept him warm. It was their only night together in the I-Hotel.

In the street, in the hall, they continued: *We won't go. Save the I-Hotel*. He had heard it all day and night. He had heard it for years, an entire life.

He had strength left to barricade the door. To block the police out. To trap themselves in. Instead, he moved away from the dresser and undid the chain above, the lock beneath.

It was 2:11 A.M., and every few seconds Vicente's arm shook and his head jerked, as though fighting in a dream. Fortunado went to him, placed his hand on his shoulder, and even after Vicente grew still he kept it there. This was the I-Hotel's final morning, so Fortunado allowed himself this moment and lay down beside Vicente, their bodies back to back, touching. Then he closed his eyes but stayed awake to make the last hours feel longer than they were.

DAYS AFTER THE TUSSLE ON the street, Vicente would tell the story to other I-Hotel tenants. "White guy, real big," he said, "and I showed him." He punched the air as he reenacted the scene, but instead of applause and admiration all he received was a warning. *Stay away from her. It's not worth the trouble*. He called them cowards and stopped telling the story.

At the Parkdale, he began taking lunch with Althea. Fortunado would catch them by the loading docks sitting together on upturned crates, sharing the butter-and-olive sandwiches she packed each day. If she worked late, Vicente insisted on waiting for her, and together they would walk to their cable car stop. Their supervisor warned them about fraternizing among staff, guests stared and whispered, but Vicente always said it: "We're not afraid."

Fortunado said nothing, swore he never would.

The heat of the summer stayed through the fall. One late Sunday night, Fortunado, Vicente, and Althea sat at a corner table in the Manila Rose Cantina beneath a slow-moving ceiling fan, trying to cool themselves with glasses of pilsner. They drank in silence, ordered more pitchers than they could finish, and when they were done Fortunado was light-headed; he could see drops of sweat fall onto the paper-covered tabletop. He hadn't felt this warm since Stockton, during those noonday hours in the fields.

Althea undid her scarf, dabbed her face and neck. "Let's go to the Dive," she said, "the three of us." Except to clean it, employees were forbidden by Parkdale policy to be near the hotel's pool, and it was close to midnight now, long past its closing. But then Althea pulled a set of keys from her purse and jangled them in the air; three times a week she collected towels from the changing rooms, and she had gone for a quick, late-night swim before. "No one will see us," she said. "No one will know."

THEY ENTERED LIKE TRESPASSERS, WENT down the back stairs to the pool. Their footsteps echoed as they walked along its blue-tiled perimeter, and the water's surface shimmered green from the lights below.

Vicente and Althea undressed and left their clothes in a neat pile on the floor. They were naked and unashamed; they had been this way before. Althea entered the pool and Vicente followed, and together they swam out, resurfacing in the deep end.

Fortunado removed his clothes. He descended the three steps into the pool, the water rising slowly to his waist, his chest. He whispered Vicente's name but heard no answer, so Fortunado took a breath and held it, submerged. He moved forward, opened his eyes, and in the watery haze he finally found Vicente, swimming beneath the surface. He had seen his body before—when he changed out of uniform at the hotel, or barged into his room to borrow a shirt—but never like this, so bare and open, arms held out as if to welcome him, to beckon. Underwater, they were the only two, with no world above to interfere, so Fortunado moved closer, unafraid. But he mistook buoyancy for the ability to swim; suddenly there was no floor beneath him, and as he sank he reached and kicked, as though trying to climb water.

It took both Vicente and Althea to bring Fortunado back to the surface, to the safety of the shallow end. They held his arms but he swiped them away, then staggered out of the pool, coughing with each breath. "I'm fine," he said, and as he gathered his clothes, he watched Vicente and Althea swim away, then disappear in a depth he would never brave again.

They finished swimming, dried themselves and dressed, hurried to the stairwell. But Vicente and Althea continued past the lobby toward the upper floors. They had planned to collect unfinished bottles of wine left outside guests' doors, and drink them in the Berlin Deluxe. "I'll see you back at the hotel," Vicente said.

"When?" Fortunado asked.

"Later tonight." Vicente looked at Althea. "Maybe tomorrow."

"You're not supposed to be there."

"No one will see us," Vicente said. "And so what if they do?"

Vicente stood four steps above but he seemed much farther, and Fortunado kept his hand tight on the rail, as if letting go meant falling. "You're not supposed to be there," he said again.

Vicente took one step down, reached for Fortunado's shoulder. "Go home," he said. Then he and Althea left, their footsteps growing fainter as they continued up the stairs.

Fortunado exited the stairwell into the empty lobby. He left the Parkdale, and walked down the long hill of Powell Street toward Manilatown. It was early Monday morning. Kearny Street was deserted. Buses had ended their run, no autos drove past, and the one other person on the street was the old Filipino sitting on his top step, staring longingly at the moon.

He entered the I-Hotel, went up to his room. He stood by his window and stared out at the blank billboard on the rooftop across, thinking about Vicente and Althea in the Berlin Deluxe, beholders of a view he could barely imagine.

. . .

ONE NIGHT A WEEK IN the Berlin Deluxe became two, sometimes three, and Vicente and Althea remained undetected. They would arrive after midnight and leave before dawn, then return in uniform to the Parkdale only hours later, ready to work. But these nights left Vicente tired, which made him tardy, and Fortunado would cover for him with flimsy excuses—a stomachache one morning, a toothache the next. Weeks of this passed, and Fortunado was done. "I won't lie for you anymore," he told Vicente. They were on the seventh floor of the Parkdale, waiting for the elevator.

"Sorry, Nado." Vicente yawned, rubbing his eyes. "I'll wake up earlier next time."

"*Next time.* Have you gone crazy? What if the boss finds you there? Or the police? What do you think they'll do to you if they find you with a white girl? This is your life, Vicente."

"The police can shoot me. Throw me in jail. I'm not afraid, either way." The elevator arrived, and they entered. "That room is good for Althea and me. A man and a woman deserve their own place."

"You're the bellboy. She's the maid. You don't live there. There's not even a bed."

"We don't *need* a bed." Vicente winked, then gave Fortunado a quick punch to the arm.

"Don't," Fortunado said.

Vicente laughed, tousled his hair, hit him again. "Stop," Fortunado said, and Vicente smiled, made another fist. But now it was Fortunado who threw a punch, one so strong that Vicente stumbled backwards, and Fortunado hit him again. Vicente got to his feet, pushed Fortunado against the wall and held him there, his hands on his collar, knuckles grazing his neck. They had not been this close for years.

"We kissed," Fortunado said. He held on to Vicente's wrists, aching to tell more: how he slept close to the wall just to hear him breathing on the other side; how he kept the tickets from the Dreamland in his pocket at all times, a memento from the night they met; how home could only be wherever Vicente was. But more words felt like drowning, so he took a breath and repeated the one thing he knew to be an undisputable truth. "We kissed."

Vicente freed his hands from Fortunado's. "Once," he said. There was no anger in his voice or on his face, only apology.

The elevator reached the lobby. The doors opened and Vicente stepped out, then closed again. Fortunado had never struck a person before, but there were times in his life he wondered what it might be like, and now he knew: the force of everything you are in a single gesture at a single moment; the hope that it will be enough and the fear that it won't. No different than a kiss.

THE PROTEST WAS FADING. FORTUNADO lay on his side facing the window, the room like a dream: for a moment, he could believe that a final night never passed, and a life in the I-Hotel never happened. *What if,* he wondered, *that was someone else?* But then he felt the slight shift of Vicente's body against his own, and Fortunado wiped his eyes and rose from the bed, put on his coat.

He gently shook Vicente's shoulder. Vicente turned toward him, blinked until he was awake.

There was no sledgehammer, no kick to the door; it simply opened, and in the hallway two officers stood, arms at their sides and no weapons in hand. "We're under orders to evict you," one of them said. "Please come with us."

Vicente stared at them, one fist closed and ready. "I don't like police," he whispered.

"They're here to help us," he said.

"We did nothing wrong."

"I know." Fortunado helped Vicente to his feet, then picked up the suitcase and led him to the door. As they passed the dresser, he reached for the envelope marked with their names, and tucked it into Vicente's coat pocket.

They stepped into the hallway. Protest signs and posters were litter now, and chains dangled from the banister and exposed pipes. An officer stood by Fortunado's door, knocked twice, then opened it. "No one here," he said. "That's everyone."

They descended the stairs, moved carefully past small desks and mattresses in their path. They reached the lobby, stepped over wood planks and broken glass, and as they crossed the fallen door of the front entrance, Fortunado took Vicente's hand. "Don't let go," he said, then led the way out of the I-Hotel.

. . .

AFTER THE FIGHT IN THE elevator, Vicente spent more nights with Althea in the Berlin Deluxe, returning to the I-Hotel only for a change of clothes. At the Parkdale, Fortunado worked the front entrance as often as he could, and whenever Vicente approached he would steer his luggage cart in another direction; after work, Fortunado would rush out to catch the next cable car back home. One night, waiting at his stop, he saw Vicente and Althea leave the Parkdale together, arms around one another as they walked down Powell Street. A light rain fell, and Vicente took off his jacket, draped it over her shoulders and held her close. They kissed.

"Disgraceful," a man with a bushy, white mustache said. He looked over at Fortunado. "You're not foolish enough to try something like that, are you, boy?"

Fortunado turned away, toward lit windows high above, and said, "No."

Hours later, alone on the third-floor fire escape of the I-Hotel, Fortunado drank through a bottle of Du Kang, remembering the kiss he shared with Vicente, how it happened in darkness, in silence. And he thought of Vicente and Althea's kiss on the sidewalk, so reckless and unhidden, which perhaps was the point: Fortunado understood how difficult love could be, how its possibility hinged on a delicate balance between complete anonymity and the undeniable need to be known.

He let the empty bottle of Du Kang roll off the fire

escape, listened for the crash of glass. The night was freezing now, and he imagined Vicente and Althea in the window of the Berlin Deluxe, looking down upon the city, warm in each other's arms.

Vicente had no right to be there; the I-Hotel was where he belonged. There were rules in this world; why should Fortunado be the only one to suffer them?

He got to his feet, steadied himself. Then he climbed inside and went downstairs, walked out of the I-Hotel to a telephone booth on the corner. He stepped in, shivering as he dialed.

The Parkdale's night operator answered.

Strangers where they didn't belong, he finally said. A couple—Filipino man, white woman—hiding in the Berlin Deluxe. Hotel security could catch them. Hurry.

He hung up the receiver, stepped out of the booth. He headed toward Market, turned east toward the water, then walked along the Embarcadero, the Bay Bridge coming into view. It was finally finished, ready for use in a matter of weeks, and all year long advertisements had announced its opening. *Joining two cities!* one poster read. *Bringing the world together!* But tonight the bridge was dark and still untraveled, and the world felt more like the place it was, an endless earth in which Fortunado stood alone.

A man in a dark suit and hat approached. He stood beside Fortunado, put his hands on the rail. "Quite a bridge," he said.

Fortunado nodded.

"Nice night, too."

Fortunado looked at the fading moon. "It's almost morning."

"There's still time," the man said. Then, without asking, he took Fortunado's hand and whispered, "It's okay. I know a place."

Fortunado looked around, checking for nearby police or anyone within earshot. When he knew it was safe, they moved away from the water to a darker, unnamed place that in daylight would be impossible to find again.

The warmth he felt inside this stranger was unquestionable and necessary, and each time it happened was meant to be the last. Now, Fortunado feared a lifetime of this and little more, and he wondered how long such a life could be.

THE NEXT MORNING FORTUNADO WAITED by his window for Vicente's return. The Parkdale would have fired Vicente, that was certain, and their security might have dragged him out of the room, down the back stairs, and thrown him into the street. When night came and he still had not returned, Fortunado picked the lock of Vicente's door, went inside, and lay on his bed. It was morning when he woke; another night without Vicente. He got up, smoothed the sheets over the mattress, and left the room as though he was never there.

At the Parkdale, none of the bellhops mentioned an incident in the Berlin Deluxe, and when Fortunado asked his boss if he had heard from Vicente, his boss said, "Maybe he had a toothache," then closed his office door. Once, he stopped in front of the Berlin Deluxe, rattled the doorknob, and whispered Vicente's name. He listened for movement, for breath, but heard nothing. After work, he checked every store, restaurant, and bar in Manilatown, even searched the crowd at the Dreamland Saloon, but the one person he recognized was the ticket man with the cane. "I know you," the old man said, and Fortunado left as quickly as he could.

Hours later, Fortunado made his way back home. When he reached the end of Kearny Street, he saw a light in Vicente's window.

He ran into the I-Hotel, up to the third floor. Without knocking he opened Vicente's door and found him sitting on the edge of his bed, elbows on his knees, hands clasped together. He was still in his uniform. "They found us," he said.

Fortunado stepped in, shut the door behind him. "When?"

"Two nights ago." He lowered his head and told Fortunado the rest, like a confession. He and Althea were sleeping when hotel security and two police officers forced the door open. They brought him to his feet, pushed him against the wall, shouted questions they wouldn't let him answer—*You think you belong here? Who do you think you are?* Althea stood in the corner, and Vicente told her not to be afraid, that nothing they did was wrong. "Then one of them, the bigger one, started shouting at her. The things he called her . . ."

He shook his head. "So I hit him. As hard as I could." He remembered Althea crying, then something smash against the back of his head, three times, maybe more. He remembered falling.

For a day and a half he sat in a cell with other men who looked the way he imagined criminals did, threatening and silent, always watching. "I didn't move. I didn't want to close my eyes. I was scared." Before they finally let him go, an officer asked if he had learned his lesson. He promised them he had.

Fortunado crossed over to the window, closed the blinds. "Althea?"

"Gone, maybe. I don't know." From the jail he rushed to Althea's boardinghouse, and the housemother told him she took the first bus back to Wisconsin, where she couldn't mix with men like him.

"You'll find her," Fortunado said.

Vicente said nothing.

Fortunado saw what looked like rings around Vicente's wrists, red as a burn. "Handcuffs," Vicente said. "They kept them on the whole time. It feels like they're still on." He put his hands, palms up, on his lap, unable to make a fist.

"You were brave, Vicente."

"I was stupid." He turned and lay on his bed, and told Fortunado to turn off the light on his way out.

Fortunado returned to his room. He sat on his bed with his back against the wall, remembering what he saw: Vicente's eye bruised purple and blue, the gash in his lower lip.

And now he could hear Vicente on the other side, turning and breathing as he tried to sleep. Once, those sounds had comforted Fortunado, made him dream of them together, holding and loving each other. But now, all he heard was loneliness, Vicente's and his own. For this, Fortunado stayed awake through the night, and wept for them both.

THOUSANDS FILLED THE STREET BUT the human barricade was gone, replaced by squads of police who fended off protesters with batons and shields, and arrested dozens more. Fortunado squeezed Vicente's hand as they moved farther out onto Kearny Street, moving in whatever direction the crowds would allow. "Almost there," Fortunado shouted, as though a true destination was finally in sight. He tightened his grip, tried to move faster, but from the side a protester rushed by, slamming into them. Fortunado fell.

The asphalt was cold against his palms, and gravel jabbed the back of his neck. Above, the sky was black and starless.

Two girls in Berkeley sweatshirts helped Fortunado to his feet. "You okay?" one asked. "Do you have someone with you?" Fortunado steadied himself, and just as he told her yes, he realized that Vicente was gone.

He could hear his name—*Nado, Nado*—but everywhere Fortunado looked he saw only strangers, hundreds of them, shouting and waving their signs. He forced his way through the crush of bodies, searching for Vicente's voice and face, until he finally reached the other side of the street. He staggered up the front stairs of an apartment building, hoping the higher ground would help him find Vicente, and from the top step he caught the flashing headlights of a white van at the end of Kearny Street. It was the shuttle for the West Oakland Senior Center, and one by one, a line of I-Hotel tenants climbed inside. As the last man boarded, Vicente approached, his feet dragging. From inside the van, tenants beckoned to him, but then Vicente stopped, let the suitcase fall from his hand. He was standing in the same spot where Fortunado had found him weeks before, asking strangers where he was, if they knew the right way home, and Fortunado remembered seeing him from afar, pacing the sidewalk corner, a man stranded on the smallest piece of land.

There was no pacing or panic now, just the stillness of a person taking in the view before him. Vicente looked at Kearny Street, watched police beat down and drag away protestors through the aimless mass, their signs fading and torn, gone. Then, as if he had finally seen enough, Vicente turned away, picked up his suitcase, and stepped into the van. Fortunado imagined him crossing the eight miles of the Bay Bridge, speeding over water as though moving from one country into the next.

The van pulled away slowly, and then it was gone.

Fortunado would make his way to the West Oakland Senior Center later; another shuttle would come. If not, then he would seek temporary shelter somewhere in the city, and find Vicente tomorrow. For now, Fortunado rested on the top step, and across the street, the I-Hotel looked like a silhouette of itself, a darkness against the city. But higher up was a last square of light, and Fortunado remembered leaving his bedside lamp on from the evening before. His was the only window lit, and in a matter of hours, daylight would make it dim and empty as all the others. But night would fall and the room would glow again, until the lamp itself finally died, or until someone turned it off.

L'amour, CA

MY SISTER, ISA, SPEAKS ENGLISH AND TAGALOG. BUT one word she could say in many languages: *koigokoro, beminnen, mahal, amor*. "It's the most important thing," she used to say, "the only thing. L-O-V-E. *Love*." So when we learned that we would be moving to California, to a city called L'amour, she called it home, the place where we were always meant to be. I believed her.

This was January of 1974, our final days in the Philippines. Isa was sixteen, I was eight, and we were from San Quinez, a small southern village surrounded by sugarcane fields and cassava groves, with a single paved road winding through. Every house was like ours, made of bamboo and nipa and built on stilts, and every neighbor was somehow family. No one was a stranger where we lived.

Like many Filipino men at the time, my father joined the U.S. Navy, and after he had served in Korea and Vietnam, his request for a transfer to America was finally granted. "Our plan from the very beginning," my father said. My mother stayed silent, rubbing the leaf of a houseplant between her fingers until it ripped. My brother, Darwin, who was twelve, said he didn't care one way or another. But Isa started packing that same day. "L'amour, L'amour," she went on, like it was the name of a special friend she had that others never would. Friends and neighbors called her haughty and boastful; our oldest cousin called her an immigrant bitch. "*American* bitch," Isa corrected her, and called our cousin a village peasant who would never know a bigger world. "You're stuck here forever." As though no place was worse than the one you were from.

This is us on the plane, the day we leave: across the aisle my mother stares ahead, barely blinking, never speaking, and my father rifles through papers, rereading each document as though he can't figure out its meaning. Darwin sleeps next to me, so deeply that I double-check the rise and fall of his chest to make sure he isn't dead. On the other side of me is Isa, and only when she looks at me do I realize I'm crying. She unbuckles my seat belt and lets me sit on her lap, promises me that I'll be fine in L'amour.

We land in San Francisco but we keep moving: as soon as we claim our boxes and bags, we board a shuttle van and head south on the freeway, turn east hours later. I'm lying down for most of the ride, my head on Isa's lap, feeling our speed. We never traveled so quickly or smoothly on the dirt roads back home; I could almost sleep. But suddenly we're slowing, and the driver yawns, "Almost there." Isa looks confused, then panicked, and when I sit up all I see are endless fields of gray stalks, the miles of freeway we leave behind, and, up ahead, we seem to be driving into a cloud. "Fog again," the driver says, and down the road, a sign becomes clearer. WELCOME TO LEMOORE, CA, it says, ENJOY YOUR STAY!

They sound the same—*L'amour, Lemoore*—but I know they're not. "Lemoore." I tug at Isa's sleeve. "What's that mean?" She doesn't answer.

We exit the freeway, turn into the Lemoore Naval Air Station. We drive through foggy streets to a section of military housing, passing rows of gray and concrete rectangular houses with low, flat roofs, then down a block that ends in a cul-de-sac. "That's ours," my father says, and we pull up to a house with a faintly lit doorway, newspaper-covered windows, a grassless yard. We step out, unload our cargo, drag boxes up the driveway to the front door. Most things are too heavy for me to lift, so I stand by the van to guard our belongings. Across the street, a balding blond man mows his dry, yellow lawn. Two houses over, a lady with a shirt that says RENO! soaps her car, sprays it down, soaps it again. Then I see a family sitting in folding lawn chairs in a line along the sidewalk, their faces toward the sky. I have never had to *meet* a person before—back home, everyone knew everyone—and now is the time for someone to say *Welcome* or *How are you?* But by the end of the day no one says hello, not even us.

I HATE MY HOUSE. TOO many walls make too many rooms, the hallway is long and dark as a tunnel. Nothing scared me back home, and I always knew where we were: you could hear a person breathe in the next room, and the floor shook when someone ascended the bamboo stairs. Now, brownish-orange carpet mutes our footsteps; I never know when a person is coming or going, who's here and who's gone.

And even our bedroom doors have locks, which we never had before. But my mother fears someone could enter the house through our bedroom windows while she's alone and cooking in the kitchen, so she makes my father reverse the bedroom doorknobs; that way, she can prevent anyone who tries to break in through our rooms from entering the rest of the house. "But I want my lock *inside* my room," Isa says, and when my father asks why, she says, "Privacy."

"And what would you be doing in there," my father says, "that you need to lock us out?" Before Isa can answer, he is kneeling on the floor, unscrewing the knob.

Strangers come each day with heavy cardboard boxes on dollies—a refrigerator one morning, a kitchen table the next. When my father breaks down the box for our new oven, I drag it to the garage and build it again, turn it on its side, and wedge it between the washing machine and the wall. I crawl in, close the flaps. I fit perfectly. Minutes pass and I decide that I'm hiding, so I wait to be found, for someone to call out, *Where are you? Where did he go?* But no one searches, even as the afternoon fades and the garage darkens.

Then someone comes. It's Isa. She has a suitcase in each hand, like she's running away. But they're empty, and she drops them to the ground like trash, pushes them against the wall with her foot. Then she paces from one end of the garage to the other, never seeing me, and stops at the driver's side window of our new, blue Impala. She stares at her reflection and sighs, then rests her forehead against the glass, clasps her hands together below her chin.

When I pray, I pray for us: my parents, Isa, Darwin, and me. Who knows what my sister prays for? When she's finished, she writes something on the window with her finger, looks it over, and hurries back inside. I wait two seconds so I won't be seen, crawl out of the box, and run to the car window, expecting a message from Isa. But all I see is her name, in fancy cursive letters, underlined twice.

I write my name over hers. I do it again and again, until all the dust is gone. Then I crawl back into my box, thinking how funny that Isa never knew I was here, that I still am.

FINALLY, WE START SCHOOL. THE morning of our first day, Darwin and I are sitting at the kitchen table, eating instant champorado from a packet, a thing I've always hated: rice boiled in chocolate has never made sense to me, and when I say, "We should have left this back there," Darwin socks me in the arm, tells me to not say things like that in front of our mother. I'm about to jab him in the head with my spoon when suddenly Isa appears in the kitchen, and the sight of her dazzles me: her eyelids are as blue as our toothpaste, her cheeks so pink I think rose petals have melted into her skin. I want to tell her, *You are beautiful!* and I'm about to, but Darwin says, "You look like a hooker," and when my mother turns from the sink and looks at Isa, I know that trouble is ahead.

She puts her hand on Isa's cheek, wipes off makeup, then rubs it between her fingers as if it were a strange kind of dust. "It's my first day," Isa says, but my mother takes her apron to Isa's face. "What will people say about you, when they see you like this? Would you do this back home?" She asks more questions, tells Isa that just because we're in Lemoore doesn't mean she can look like any girl on the street, and she's wiping makeup from Isa's face the whole time, until nothing is left. When my mother is done, she steps backwards, leans against the sink. "Go to school," she tells us. She doesn't walk us to the door. She doesn't say goodbye.

We walk out of the house, down the driveway, and out of the cul-de-sac. The sun fades as the fog ahead thickens, and our windbreakers don't keep us warm. "Walk faster," Darwin says, blowing on his hands and rubbing them together. We lose him a block later—his school is in another direction—and when he leaves, he just shrugs and says bye, his teeth still chattering. Isa and I go on, holding hands even more tightly now.

Kids crowd the front steps of my school. Isa leads us through the building, down a hallway to my classroom. The door is barely open. We go in. We find rows of empty desks, blank chalkboards, and no teacher in sight. "Maybe we shouldn't be here."

"No," Isa says, double-checking the room number, "this is right." She bends down to fix my collar, promises that everything about this day will be fine, then looks at the clock above the chalkboard beside the American flag. I look too, thinking about the distance between Lemoore and San Quinez, how here it's today and there it's tomorrow, but the arms of the clock don't move, not at all. I don't know how to tell time, but I understand that Isa is late and not ready for today. Her windbreaker looks like a plastic trash bag on her body, her face is smeary and gray.

The bell rings. Isa leaves. Kids come running in and around me to their desks, and finally the teacher appears with a stickpin between her fingers. "Wear this," she tells me, pinning a name tag shaped like an apple onto my shirt, then leads me to the front of the class. She stands behind me with her hands tight on my shoulders, telling everyone how far I have traveled, and how lucky we are to be together. Then I tell them what my father told us all to say on our first day: "I am very happy to be here." Two girls giggle and won't stop, and when the teacher asks what's so funny, one says that I said *bery* instead of *very*. So I repeat myself, and now I hear it too. *Bery. Bery.* Back home, my English was perfect; here, I can't get it right. I don't speak the rest of the day.

After school, I watch a janitor sweep the hallway while I wait for Isa outside my classroom. When she arrives, she says nothing, doesn't even ask me how I am, or how my day has been. "Let's go home" is all she says, then turns, exits the school. She stays ahead of me the entire way, her legs so long and fast that I can't keep up, and when I almost do, I catch glimpses of her face, her teary forward stare. *Why do you cry, Isa?* I want to ask. *Did they laugh at you, too?* But before I can get a question out, I fall behind again. Half a block separates us by the time we reach our street, and when I'm finally home, Isa is already in her room, door closed and the radio blaring. In the living room, Darwin is lying on the floor in front of the TV, and in the kitchen my mother is staring at a boiling pot, her arms folded over her chest. When I tell them I'm home, they barely nod. So I go back to the garage and crawl into the box, practicing the word *very* over and over until evening, and time for us to eat.

The next day is not much different. All through class I'm silent, and I spend recess lining up pebbles along the bottom of the playground fence. What saves me from tears is knowing that the school day will end, and that Isa will come for me.

Some better days are ahead. Like those afternoons when Isa picks me up wearing school-spirit chains around her neck, or the time she wandered into a picture on the front page of the school newspaper. Once, I even catch her writing *Isa, Class of '75* on the palm of her hand, as if she has always been and will always be a part of them. But when school is over, the autograph pages in her yearbook are empty and white. No one wished her a happy summer, or good luck for the following year. And though her name is listed in the index, my sister is nowhere in the book.

. . .

EARLY JUNE. SUMMER VACATION, AND the days drag.
Isa is always lying on her bed listening to the radio, and the
thump of Darwin's basketball is like the ticking of a slow-
moving clock. I spend my time by the living room window,
watching kids bicycle and roller-skate by, chasing each other
down with water pistols. Once, two kids walking a wolf-
faced dog stop in front of our house, and just as I'm about
to wave, they shout, *"Vietnamese people eat dogs!"* so I yell back,
"We're not Vietnamese people!" then shut the window and draw
the curtains.

Then something happens: one night at dinner, Isa
announces that she's been hired as a cashier at Lanes, the
diner inside the Naval Station bowling alley. "It's summer-
time," she says, "maybe I should work." My mother says no,
but my father says (quietly, like he's embarrassed), "We need
the money," and he allows Isa to take the job on one condition: Darwin and I must accompany her each day, and stay
with her until my father comes for us in the evening. "A girl
shouldn't be out there alone," he says. But Isa insists she'll
be fine on her own, that nothing is dangerous in Lemoore.
"Please let me have this," she says. When no one answers,
she goes to the window above the sink, slides it open. "Tell
me what's out there. Tell me what to be afraid of." She looks
like she might cry.

My father tells Isa to take her seat and finish her dinner.
Isa sits, arms folded across her chest. I put my hand on Isa's

to comfort her, but now I'm wondering: When did she go to the bowling alley? Did she tell me she was leaving, but somehow I forgot?

"Let *go*," Isa says to me.

The morning Isa starts her job, I find her in the bathroom, trying on her uniform, a mustard-colored bowling shirt with matching slacks, and orange shoes that fail to give her the height she'd hoped for. She checks herself in the mirror, moving her shoulders forward, then back, shifting her waist to the right, to the left. "What do you think," she asks me. "Do I look like Cheryl Tiegs?"

"You look like Nora Aunor." Darwin laughs, walking by the bathroom. "You look like Vilma Santos." He goes on with a list of the corniest Filipina actresses, and Isa gets so mad she douses him with a Dixie cup full of bright blue toilet water. "Immigrant bitch!" he shouts.

"*American* bitch," I correct him.

Isa bends down, puts her hand on my cheek, and says, "I love you."

After breakfast, my father drops us off at the bowling alley. Before Isa can get out of the car, he grabs hold of her wrist. "This is a good opportunity for you," he tells her, "so work hard, and be good. And you two"—he looks at Darwin and me—"watch your sister." But as soon as my father drives off, three boys approach on bikes, and Darwin high-fives each one. They're friends from his school and he goes off with them, tells us he'll be back when my father picks us up in the afternoon. "Have fun being bored," he says. Every day after, he leaves us.

So from the beginning, I am the watcher of Isa and this is what I do: each morning when we arrive, I take a corner booth and watch her ring up meals and wipe tabletops and counters, all day long. I know she wishes I weren't there, so I stay quiet and still as I can, but after a week, I'm a problem. "He's here again," Isa's boss says. "Why is he always here?" Isa moves her arm in fast circles as she wipes off a nearby table, as if she is trying to come up with a story for me. I give her one. "Our mother is dead!" I shout this out to make sure Isa's boss hears me. "No one is home to take care of me!" Isa looks up. I try winking at her but instead I blink, and suddenly tears I didn't plan come streaming.

"I'm sorry," he says, patting Isa on the shoulder. "Sorry." That day, he tells Isa to keep all the money in the tip jar, and says I can eat all the corn dogs and Eskimo Pies I want.

We never talk about the lie. Once it's out, I can't take it back. And why should I? My mother takes good care of us—food is always on the table, our clothes are always clean—but the rest of the time she's sitting in her room, reading and rereading letters that make her weep. When we come home, she never asks how we are, or how we've been, and when I ask about her day, she just says, "You were gone. I was alone."

It's better here with Isa. She smiles for me at least, like when she spells my name in ketchup over a basket of fries, or when old ladies call her "dear" and remark on her beauty and good English. One day Isa tells a customer, "Thank you for coming to Lanes," and she sounds so pleased and finally fulfilled with our life in Lemoore that I need to hear it again. So I run out into the bowling alley to the pay phone by the bathroom, drop a dime, and call the diner.

Isa picks up. "Thank you for calling Lanes," she says.

I whisper, "It's me." I can see her but she can't see me, even as I wave. "It's me," I say again.

"Who?"

We have never spoken on the phone before—we have never been apart—and now I sound like a stranger. "Hello?" she says, turning side to side, as though the person on the other end is somehow with her in the room.

Before she asks who I am again, I hang up and go back, running.

Bowling-alley days get longer, I keep watching Isa, and nothing happens. So, little by little, I start to leave. At first I stick close by the diner door, watching off-duty soldiers bowl, and I cheer their strikes and laugh at their gutter balls. Then I walk my fingers along the racks of bowling balls, looking for ones I can lift. I start to go farther: without coins I go to the arcade and pretend to play pinball, or finish abandoned games of air hockey. I like to push buttons and pull knobs on the vending machines, hoping that gum or a bag of chips will fall for free, and one day a roll of Life Savers actually does. I snatch it, look around to check if anyone saw, then run back to the diner to tell Isa about my incredible luck and share my candy with her. But when I get to the diner, Isa isn't at the register or standing behind the counter. Instead, she's in a booth by the jukebox, sitting across from someone, a boy her age, a boy with long white arms full of freckles and the reddest hair I have ever seen.

I press my hands and face against the glass door. I watch. They're just talking, that's all, but he's holding a cigarette, and when he reaches to move a strand of hair from Isa's face, she flinches, just a little. He keeps his hand there, even as the cigarette burns. I haven't seen anyone touch my sister's face since my mother, months before, the morning we started school.

HIS NAME IS MALCOLM AND he's always here. He bowls all morning in the very last lane, then visits Isa at noon, stays until we have to leave. He never brings flowers and they never kiss, but, once, they disappear. Returning from the arcade, I find a note taped to the cash register that says BACK IN TEN MINUTES. But I don't know how long ten minutes is, and despite the clock above the jukebox I still don't know how to tell time. So I go running out the diner, to the arcade, the women's bathroom, then the diner again, and when there is still no sign of Isa, I run out into the parking lot, up and down the rows of cars. The daylight is so bright I can barely see, and every direction I go in is wrong. But finally I find her, sitting on the rear bumper of a sky blue van, right next to Malcolm. A cigarette burns between her fingers.

I point at her to make her understand: *You were gone! I couldn't find you!* but I'm crying too hard and can't catch my breath. She takes my hand and pulls me close, kisses my cheeks, my nose, the top of my head. "Watch," she says. She takes the cigarette to her lips, closes her eyes like she's gathering courage, and exhales a wave of smoke. "See?" She opens her eyes. I breathe her smoke through my nose, and when it makes me sneeze, Isa starts laughing, Malcolm too, and now so do I. "More," I say, and now Isa is making smoke rings, a thing I've never seen, and I try to break them with my finger before they float away and vanish.

Who knew a person could form circles from smoke? Or cry and laugh at the same time? This is a day of learning new things: I look at Isa looking at me, and I think we are amazing.

Later, when my father picks us up, I tell him, "Nothing happened today," then get into the backseat with Isa, put my head on her lap. I watch her staring out the window, and when she looks down at me, she smiles and sighs, like her longing has ended, and we have finally arrived in the place we were meant to be.

MIDDLE OF AUGUST. EIGHT MONTHS in America, and Isa will be seventeen. The year before, the whole village celebrated her birthday, and in her white, floor-length dress, Isa looked like a bride. This year, we celebrate at the new Pizza Hut on base, and give small gifts: she gets pink fuzzy slippers from my parents, nothing from Darwin, and an egg-carton caterpillar I made in school, from me. "Next year you'll get more," my father says, almost whispering, and just as I'm about to sing "Happy Birthday," my mother shushes me. "People will stare at us," she says. When I try again, Isa takes my hand. "You'll sing to me later," she says. But I never do.

The one who makes her birthday matter is Malcolm. The next day at the diner, he tells Isa he wants to take her out for her birthday, someplace far away from here. "Hanford," he says, "maybe Fresno. Anywhere but Lemoore." He takes the saltshaker and taps grains onto the table. "Goddamn Lemoore."

Isa puts her hand on his wrist, right in front of me. "But Lemoore means love," she says. "In French." Then she says "love" all the other ways she knows—*koigokoro, beminnen, mahal*— and Malcolm lights a cigarette, nodding with every word.

That night at dinner, Isa says her boss needs her for a Friday-night late shift and will pay her double, maybe triple, even drive her home afterward. She says the late shift might lead to a promotion, maybe a raise, but my mother says no. "A girl out at night," she says, doom and threat in her voice.

"Then I'll be with her," I say. I tell my parents how much Isa's boss adores me, how I remind him of his son. "But that boy died. A car crash," I say. "He was crossing the street. A van came . . ." The story is even better than we rehearsed it, and as I lie I'm picturing Isa in a car at night with the window rolled down, her ponytail like a ribbon in the wind, singing to any song the radio plays, and finally, because a dead child fills them with pity, my parents tell us yes, we can go, just this once. "Thank you," Isa says to them, but she's really thanking me. Beneath the table I squeeze her hand to tell her, *You're welcome*.

Everything is perfect. Darwin has come down with a fever and won't be coming with us. My mother still refuses to leave the house at night, and insists my father stay with her. "We'll be okay," I tell my parents throughout the day. "We take care of each other." They believe whatever I say.

Just before dark, my father drives us to the bowling alley. Before we get out, he makes us kiss him goodbye on the cheek, which we've never done the other times he drops us off. He drives away, and I imagine myself in his rearview mirror, shrinking and shrinking as he travels down the road. I'm still waving even after he's gone.

Isa hurries inside to change in the bathroom. I stay where I am. Then, as if he'd been watching, Malcolm pulls up in his van. He doesn't say hello, doesn't invite me in. He just sits there smoking a cigarette, then flicks it out the passenger window. I watch it glowing on the ground until Isa steps out and takes my hand.

"Let's get him home," Malcolm says. He reaches over and opens the passenger door. The backseat is crammed with boxes and crates, album sleeves, parts of a bike, so I sit in front on Isa's lap. She goes over the plan once more, making sure I remember every step. Her arms are wrapped around my chest and I lean back, my head resting against her shoulder. She's shivering and her knee bounces a little, like a mother trying to calm the wailing baby in her arms. "I'll be fine," I whisper, and Isa says, "I know."

Off we go. Malcolm takes a different route home, and every turn becomes a street I don't know. When we finally reach the end of our block, the fog is so thick I almost don't recognize that this is where we live.

Malcolm pulls over. Isa and I step out. "Count eleven houses," she says, pointing toward home, "and you'll be there." She pulls my hood over my head, tugs at the draw-strings, and as she knots them together she tells me to be brave, though she is the one who cries. Then she tells me that she loves me, and that's the most important thing, the only thing.

She kisses my cheek, then steps back, climbs into the van. I let them leave first, watching the red taillights of Malcolm's van until they disappear into the fog, and that's when I see it, for the very first time: my breath in the air. It floats before my eyes like a tiny ghost, and I'm so amazed that I must stand still, marveling at the fact that I possess the power to project something from deep inside me into the night air. I breathe again, watching my breath and remembering the smoke rings Isa made, and I think we are exactly the same.

I start toward home, counting off houses. I walk up someone's driveway, and though the garage is padlocked shut, I tug at the handle anyway, as though it might open. Then I run a zigzag line from house to house, breathing hard so my breath floats in the air again, and no one ever sees me. I've never been outside by myself like this, so late at night in Lemoore. I'm so brave that I even walk in the middle of the street and shout, just once, *"Hello!"*

I stop at the bottom of our driveway. The living room window glows blue and I move toward it slowly, staying low. I stick close to the wall, peeking in. Darwin is on the floor wrapped in a blanket, my father dozes on his recliner, my mother leans against the doorway of the kitchen. Even as I move to the center of the window, they still think I'm gone.

My breath fogs the glass. It's cold. I leave my family and hurry over to the side of the garage, find the key and flashlight we hid behind the trash cans, and let myself in, make my way quietly and slowly to my box. I crawl inside. In the corner is a pack of crayons and two foil-wrapped corn dogs from Lanes, a thermos of juice, and the roll of Life Savers that fell for free. Next to it is Isa's watch. She'll be home by 2 A.M., when she'll come into the garage, get me from the box, and together we will enter the house, as if we were never apart. I look at the watch. I see the 2, but I don't know how long I'll have to wait. I don't even know the time now.

I stand the flashlight on its end. The whole box glows. I take a red crayon to draw a picture of Isa's night out, but I'm not sure what's beyond Lemoore, maybe lit-up cities with high-rising buildings, strangers who wave and say *Welcome*, and tell you their names. So, instead of Isa's story, I start drawing ours instead: with a blue crayon I make a circle for our cul-de-sac, and inside it I draw five people in a row, tallest to shortest. Then I surround the circle with stars, and I decide our cul-de-sac is the whole world itself, our bodies so big we fill it, as if we are everywhere at once.

THERE IS A LINE OF morning light beneath the garage door when I open my eyes, just enough to help me find my way into the house.

Isa didn't wake me. Maybe she forgot. I go to her bedroom door. I whisper her name and wait for her to whisper mine, so we both know we're here. But there's only silence, and the outside knob is still locked, so I unlock it and step inside. Her bed is still made.

She's not hiding in the closet or under the bed. She's not in the living room, or the kitchen, or the bathroom, and now I'm thinking that I've messed up, that she's on her way home, and I came back too soon. Everyone still sleeps, and I don't know what to do. I climb on top of her bed, wait for her all over again.

I wake the second time to shouting and panic, to my father's face in mine. My mother is behind him, and Darwin is in the hallway, shivering with fever. "What happened last night? What have you done?" My father is shaking me, harder and harder. "Where is your sister?" But I have nothing to tell. All I prepared for was Isa's return, so I wait for it, refusing to speak, even if he hits me.

The answers come, later that night, when Isa calls from a pay phone in a place she won't name, to tell us she's not coming back, that she's sorry but happier this way, that she is with Malcolm and she is in love. I'm listening to this on the telephone in my parents' room, my hand cupped over the receiver so they won't know I'm here.

ISA IS GONE, AND NOW the house feels too small. No matter where I go, I can hear my parents fight, shouting things I shouldn't know—that my mother never wanted to leave, that my father wishes he was alone in America, free of the worries we cause. *"Our plan,"* she says one night. "Is this what we planned for?" My father doesn't answer. He just stands there, jangling his car keys in his pocket, as if he could leave at any moment.

Darwin never mentions Isa, but once I catch him bouncing his basketball outside Isa's window, staring in. When he sees me, he pops me with the ball so hard that I fall backwards to the ground. He walks off, and when I breathe, I hurt.

Isa doesn't call again. We go for help, but the Navy can do nothing. Neither can the police. She's gone, not missing, is what they tell us. I don't know the difference.

We do what we can. One morning, my mother and I go door-to-door through the neighborhood looking for her, but she makes me do the talking. "Did you see my sister?" I'll ask a neighbor, then hold up a picture of Isa on her sixteenth birthday. Sometimes I catch my mother peering into their living rooms, her head turning slowly from side to side, like she is trying to learn how other people live. No one has seen Isa, but we go house to house with her picture the next day and the day after, and people start to know who we are.

My father searches at night. Once, he lets me go with him. I sit in the back, kneeling on the seat with my chin on the headrest, looking out the rear window. We drive for what feels like hours, up and down the same streets over and over, until finally we are outside of town on a long, two-lane road. Suddenly he pulls to the side, and when I turn my father is leaning back, his hands still on the wheel. "I don't know where we are," he says to himself. But I do, only now the fog is gone, the gray stalks are green and sprouting corn, and behind us is a row of palm trees, almost as tall as the ones back home.

Sooner or later, we stop searching. I don't know when, I don't know why, but my parents decide that we must learn to live this way, and one night at dinner, I find only four settings on the table. "If she wants us, she'll call," my father says, scooping rice onto his plate. And, just like that, things go back to normal: my father sleeps early again to rest for the next day's work, my mother cooks and cleans, Darwin plays basketball and rides bikes with his friends. The busier we stay, the less my parents fight, the less Darwin bullies me, and soon, school begins again. I'm a third grader now, learning things all the time: that our final states are Alaska and Hawaii, that anything times zero equals zero. One morning I wake up and my mother tells me, "You're nine years old today."

Days feel fuller than they ever were, and after dinner, when everyone is tired and almost ready for bed, we gather in the living room, in front of the new TV. It's color but still secondhand, and one night half the picture comes in lines so wavy that they almost hurt my eyes. So I look away toward the window, remembering myself on the other side of the glass, the way I watched my family as they are now: nonmoving and silent, their faces blank and glowing blue from the TV screen. We couldn't be truly happy, but somehow everyone rests easy, as if the fact that we are four instead of five is simply a number, and not a tragedy. No one even cries, and I can't understand why.

I put my head on my knees, close my eyes. Somewhere, Isa is fine without us; here, we are fine without Isa. And this is the truth I don't want to know: that the ones who leave and the ones who get left keep living their lives, whatever the distance between. But not me. When I was outside in the night, I watched my family; I knew they were fine. When she thought she was alone, I watched Isa; I listened to her pray. For the rest of my life, I would be like this. It's the difference, I think, between all of them and me; even when I was gone, I was here.

IN THE LAST HOURS OF the school day, during filmstrips about good hygiene, our forefathers, and California history, I daydream of Isa: she zooms down a highway edged with cornfields that become skyscrapers, her face framed in the passenger window of Malcolm's van. Wherever she goes, strangers bid her hello, and I think of her thinking of us: that we're stuck here forever, that we will never know a bigger world.

After school, walking home, I daydream again, always of reunion: I'm at the end of our block when I see her, standing at the bottom of the driveway. At first she can't see me in the fog, but then I emerge from it, and now I'm running to her and she's running to me.

It never happens this way.

In December, on the last day of school before winter vacation, I've just walked in the door when my father calls out from the kitchen. "Come here," he says, and before I can ask why he's home so early, I see Isa sitting in her chair at the table. Her eyes are pink from crying, her lips are pressed together like she's keeping a secret. "Hug your sister," my mother says, so I move closer to Isa, who stares at her lap and whispers "Sorry," over and over. Her face seems wider now, heavier, and one thick strand of hair crosses her forehead and trails down her shoulder to her elbow. I rub it between my fingers, wondering how long it took to grow, and I think I might understand the way time works: how its passing is impossible to see, but when it's gone, you feel it. "You should cut this," I say. Then I do as I'm told and embrace my sister, and that's when I see it: the dome of her belly, bigger than it was the last time we held each other.

THIS IS ISA'S STORY: MALCOLM got her pregnant. He didn't want the baby, and then he didn't want her. He paid for a bus ticket from wherever they were to Lemoore, and sent Isa on her way. That's all she told my parents; I never knew more than that. "But you shamed us," my father tells her in a voice so soft he sounds like he's speaking to the dead. "You shamed yourself. And if he shows up at my door—"

"He won't," Isa says, and she's right: I never see Malcolm again and he never calls, but now a baby is inside my sister. I think of its curled-up and freckled body, and wonder what will happen when it's born. Do I feed it when it's hungry? Hold it when it cries? No one talks about it, prepares me for it. This baby is like being in America—a thing that just happens, a thing you learn to live with.

My mother is proof of this. One afternoon I'm lying on my bedroom floor staring at the ceiling when I hear her humming. I run to her room, find her laying out baby clothes, their tiny sleeves and pant legs splayed out like *X*'s across her bed. "You wore these once," she says, then holds the smallest shirt I have ever seen against my chest. "Now look. How big you are." She breathes deeply, sits on the edge of her bed, puts her fingers on my cheek.

"Isa left us," I tell her, in case she forgot.

I haven't hugged or kissed Isa since she's been back. Whole days pass and I won't even say hello. She is the same way, and she joins us only at the dinner table, where all she does is stare at some spot on the table or the wall. Once, her stare is so long and steady she barely blinks, barely breathes, and I get suspicious: maybe she misses wherever she was, and is planning to leave us again.

I slam my hand on the table to bring her back. The forks and spoons rattle on our plates.

"Are you brain-damaged?" Darwin says, and when he kicks me hard under the table, I don't even flinch.

Days before Christmas, at the start of each night, the neighborhood houses glow and blink with colored lights, but ours is dim and plain. "They don't have Christmas trees back home," my father says one morning. "Maybe we should get one?"

They shop for a tree that afternoon, and as they pull out of the driveway I go running to my father's window. "I'll watch Isa," I say. But he barely nods, like he knows I'll fail again.

After they leave, Darwin goes outside to shoot baskets, and I sit in the dark hallway, on the floor in front of Isa's open door. She hasn't felt well all day, so she lies on her bed, facing the wall. But we are alone in the house, just Isa and me, and now is the time for all my questions—where she was all those months and the things she did; if she dreamed of me as often as I dreamed of her; and did she plan, from the very beginning, to leave us, knowing that I would wait for her, inside a box?

"You were gone" is the first thing I say.

She nods her head.

"When you left, nobody talked to me. For a long time. Even though I was here." I stare at the carpet, dig my finger into it. "We drove at night to find you. We couldn't." Outside, Darwin's basketball thumps and thumps, and I dig my finger deeper and deeper. "I walk by myself now. All the way to school. All the way home." When Isa turns to face me, I realize I'm crying, but I keep going, telling her more she doesn't know about me: new words I've learned in school, the teeth I've lost, how now I'm nine years old and can finally say *very* the way you're supposed to, but despite all these facts I always end up saying the same thing: "You were gone."

"But I'm back," she says, trying to smile. "I'm here." She takes a deep breath, sits up, rubbing her sides like the baby takes up too much room inside her. Slowly, she gets to her feet, reaches into her dresser, and from beneath folded dresses she takes out a cigarette and a book of matches. She lights it, breathes deeply, and a ring of smoke floats toward me. "Remember how much you liked these? How they made you laugh?" She breathes and breathes, and more rings float my way, but I let them fade.

She doesn't give up. She takes the cigarette to her lips, takes a long, deep breath, but instead of smoke rings all that comes out is a cough. She tries once more but coughs again, like she's forgotten how to smoke. She stubs out the cigarette against the window screen, sets the butt on the sill, and now she hunches over, holding her belly as though it's suddenly heavier than it was before. "I don't feel right," she says, squinting with pain. She steps toward the bed, sits but misses the edge, falls to the floor. She looks funny and I almost laugh, but then I hear her say, "It hurts," and when she looks down between her legs, spots of blood are on her pink pajama bottoms. She puts her hand there, then looks at the blood on her fingers. "Something's wrong," she says. She tries to stand, but she hurts too much to move.

I get up, step into her room, reach for the box of tissues on her dresser and try handing it to her. But she pushes it away and asks for our mother, our father, then says she should get to a hospital, and now I think this baby will be born now, here. But I'm not ready. I don't want to be.

I pull out a tissue and lay it down by her hand. I tell her I'll get Darwin, that he will know what to do. "Just wait here, okay?" I close the door, tell her not to leave, and then, in case she tries to, I lock it.

I take a step back and listen to her shouting my name. Then the doorknob rattles, and I imagine what my mother feared: a stranger on the other side, trying to break in. "Just wait," I say again, then run to the end of the hallway. "I'll be back." Behind me, I can hear Isa's hand slapping softly against the door.

I head to the living room and walk out of the house. I go down the driveway past Darwin, who keeps bouncing his basketball against the garage door. "Where are you going?" he says, but I keep walking, even when he tells me to stay.

I continue down the sidewalk, count eleven houses. When I reach the end, I cross the street, and at the next house a lady is in the front window, holding a teacup in her hand. She sees me standing at the bottom of her driveway, but instead of drawing the curtain or looking away, she just waves, takes a sip of her drink. I don't wave back or even smile, but I nod to let her know I see her.

Then I turn back toward my street. Night is starting, but the air is warm, all the rooftops blink with colored lights, and Christmas trees full of ornaments and silvery tinsel light up every living room window. Soon, our house will be this way too.

This is what L'amour was meant to be. This is the place my sister called home. Finally, after a long, long year, we're here. And so I go back, walking first, then running fast because I can't wait to ask her, *Isa, how are you? Isa, how have you been?*

ACKNOWLEDGMENTS

FOR THE GIFTS OF TIME, FINANCIAL SUPPORT, AND community during the writing of this book, I'm grateful to the Wallace Stegner Program at Stanford University, the University of Oregon Creative Writing Program, the George Bennett Fellowship at Phillips Exeter Academy, the James McCreight Fellowship at the Wisconsin Institute for Creative Writing, the John Steinbeck Fellowship at San Jose State University, Saint Mary's College of California (especially the Department of English, the MFA Program in Creative Writing, and the Faculty Development Committee), the MacDowell Colony, the Corporation of Yaddo, the Headlands Center for the Arts, the Jacob K. Javits Fellowship Program, the Elizabeth George Foundation, the National Endowment for the Arts, and the Mrs. Giles Whiting Foundation.

Thanks to Ira Silverberg, for keeping faith in my work, and to Ruth Curry and Dwight Curtis, who helped take care of it. C. Michael Curtis and Maria Streshinsky at *The*

Atlantic, Michael Ray at *Zoetrope: All-Story,* Frank Stewart and Leigh Saffold at *Manoa,* and Don Lee and Gish Jen at *Ploughshares* kindly published these stories, and the good people at Ecco/HarperCollins, especially Lee Boudreaux, my truly excellent editor, and Abigail Holstein, turned them into a book. Thank you all.

To the friends who read these stories when they were barely readable—Otis Haschemeyer, Jack Livings, Katharine Noel, Tamara Guirado, Julie Orringer, Adam Johnson, ZZ Packer, Edward Schwarzschild, Angela Pneuman, Tom Kealey, Tom McNeely, James Pearson, Cai Emmons, Paige Newman, Natasha Garber, Melanie Conroy-Goldman, Rosemary Graham, and Anthony Doerr—I owe you all a drink.

For their wisdom and generosity, I'm grateful to my teachers Chang-rae Lee, Peter Ho Davies, Rebecca Stowe, Tobias Wolff, John L'Heureux, Elizabeth Tallent, and Bharati Mukherjee.

Thanks to Tara Runyan, who read from the beginning, and to Serena Crawford, who read to the end.

And to Bruce, who arrived just in time.

Finally, my gratitude and love to my family: my nieces and nephews, who make me laugh; my brothers and sisters (all eight), who work harder than anyone I know; and my mom and dad, who brought us home.